Zoey's Zany Life

Mikayla

Zoey's Zany Life

* *
* *

Mikayla Lowery

CHARLIE'S PORT PRESS / ATLANTA

Charlie's Port Press

9305 Bluejack Lane

Roswell, GA 30076

www.charliesport.org

Publisher's Note: This is a work of fiction. Names, characters, places, and incidents are a product of the author's imagination. Locales and public names are sometimes used for atmospheric purposes. Any resemblance to actual people, living or dead, or to businesses, companies, events, institutions, or locales is completely coincidental.

Book design © 2017 BookDesignTemplates.com

Cover design © 2017 Ben Curtis Jones / www.bencurtisjones.com

Ordering Information: Special discounts are available on quantity purchases by corporations, associations, and others. For details, contact the publisher at the address above.

Zoey's Zany Life / Mikayla Lowery — First Edition

ISBN 978-0-692-90898-3

Printed in the United States of America for distribution in the U.S. / Canada / UK / Europe / Australia

Contents

For my Nana, "Joyce Biddulph", a three-time cancer survivor. One of the strongest people I know. She gave me my love of reading and has always shown unconditional love and support in all I do.

1

The Switch

MY name is Zoey Grace Song. It was day 67 of our 180-day school year, and sixth grade was not turning out to be the year I thought it would be. Mrs. Lewis was lecturing me about using 100 words to answer a question, saying I talk way too much and that my answer was "irrelevant" because I mentioned my Aunt Agnes, my favorite song, my love for pancakes and, okay, several other topics. I am not one for short answers. I like to hear myself talk. I just can't help it. So I landed in detention that afternoon, my own *private* detention, because Mrs. Lewis said she didn't want me to talk to anyone else. She actually said, "Why can't you be more like Zelena?"

Zelena is my twin sister. People say she's too quiet, but I don't think so. Her full name is Zelena Marie Song. I also have a brother named Zach. He's 16 but will soon turn 17. His full name is Zachary Zane Song. Anyway, I had to sit by myself in detention for an entire hour! I guess it wasn't so bad. I talked to myself. It was a great conversation. Sometimes people can talk too much, but I don't think I'm one of those people.

Because of detention, I had to walk home from school. I normally take the bus. I wasn't looking forward to telling my mom about detention. When I got home she said, "Zoey Song, were you given detention again?"

"Who told you? Wait, was it Zelena?" I always ask questions and answer them before anyone else can.

Mom said, "No, Mrs. Lewis called me. You better stop talking so much in class; it keeps getting you into trouble."

"Yes, ma'am. But it's impossible to give a short answer. I only give short answers when I finally get *into* trouble!" Mom sent me directly to my room with an order to complete homework without dinner. I sank into bed, longing for her spicy meatball veggie soup. It is totes delish!

Multiple-choice questions are my least favorite type of test or homework, because it is really about *minimal* choices. How can I express myself with minimal choices? Mom, however, likes for me to have the multiple-choice format, because once when I was writing an answer it took up two pages. So now she checks my homework. I'm in the sixth grade and can still get distracted while reading fourth grade books. I want to be able to talk to the book.

I thought about what Mrs. Lewis said, which is weird because I don't usually think about what other people say. I wondered if Mrs. Lewis would like me better if I was like

Zelena? She *is* my twin. I pondered about how I could switch places with Zelena until I had a plan!

"Zelena!" I shouted when she walked in the door. "Would you like to help me out tomorrow and switch places with me? I know you have to volunteer at 'Help Keep Houston Clean', but this is really important."

"I guess so. Besides, tomorrow at 'Help Keep Houston Clean' we are cleaning the sewers. So good luck with that," Zelena joked.

*
* *

The next day Zelena wore my shirt that said ZOEY and I wore her shirt that said ZELENA. On the bus, my friend Sarah sat next to Zelena, whom everyone thought was me. Sarah said, "Hi Zoey, how was detention?"

Zelena quietly said, "Uh, it was okay."

Sarah asked, "Do you have a sore throat?" with concern.

Zelena said, "No."

Sarah rolled her eyes. "Finally she's quiet."

"Later, when Zelena entered Mrs. Lewis' room for first period, Mrs. Lewis looked her directly in the eye and said, "You."

Zelena innocently answered, "Me?"

Mrs. Lewis said, "Yes, you! You better not cause any more trouble."

Zelena said, "Yes ma'am," with fear in her voice and quickly sat down at my desk while I sat at hers.

Mrs. Lewis said, "Good morning class. I hope everyone has read the book I assigned *The Tell Tale Heart*. Can anyone tell me what they learned from it?"

I raised my hand. Mrs. Lewis said, "Zelena."

Then I realized I was supposed to be Zelena and said, "Umm-can I go to the restroom?" instead of giving what Mrs. Lewis calls an "irrelevant" answer. It was only first period and it was getting hard. Instead of going to art next, I had to go to Zelena's advanced science class. Instead of drawing my favorite animals like zebras, I was stuck dissecting a frog. Yuck! I have always loved drawing. Art is so much fun. But I suddenly remembered that my art class was showing our work to our parents. Then I realized my parents would find out about Zelena and me switching places!

Meanwhile, looking at my frog I noticed his skin was plain and regular looking, boring and green. Then I saw a beaker full of a blue chemical. I thought, *hmmm*. No one has ever seen a blue-skinned frog. So I decided to put the skin in the blue chemical filled beaker.

Ms. Adams Yelled, "NOOOOOO!" and ran over to stop what I was about to do, but it was too late. The blue chemical exploded everywhere leaving a huge blue mess that smelled awful. Ms. Adams ordered that I clean up the mess and march to the principal's office.

As I walked through the hallway people laughed at the blue frog skin that was all over me. I had to face the music when I reached the principal's office, and it was not a pretty song.

To my surprise, Zelena was in the principal's office too. *What could she have done?* The principal wasn't there yet so I asked Zelena, "Why are you here?"

Before she could answer, in came Principal Ruff. Even her name sounds cruel, and her voice sent chills up my back. "Yes, Zelena, why are you here? When I heard that you were coming to the office covered in blue frog skin, I thought something was suspicious. Now I get it! You two switched places again!"

I said, "I am so sorry!"

Principal Ruff said, "You should be. You now have you *and* your sister in trouble." I felt really bad. Principal Ruff then said, "Zelena, you have detention for one week. Zoey, you have detention for the rest of the month. Starting right *now*! You will start by scraping gum off all the desks in the entire school."

I ran out of the room as fast as I could. I couldn't believe I had detention for a month. I got the supplies I needed for scraping gum and went to work. It was a disgusting job. One of the pieces of gum even had a tooth! I put it in my pocket to see if the tooth fairy would still come. What a score! But I was not happy. Principal Ruff was probably telling my parents what trouble I had caused as I scraped away.

After I was finished, I got an awful gum scraping cramp. I went to the parking lot where my family was waiting. It was silent in the car, and I knew they were mad.

"You have every right to be mad," I started.

Mom spoke the dreaded words, "We are not mad. Just disappointed."

Disappointment feels worse than anything in the world.

* * *

When we got home, Mom gave Zelena and I bracelets that had our first names engraved. I was surprised mom had gotten us a gift when we had just gotten in so much trouble, but then I realized the bracelets could only be removed from our wrists by a key; a key that Mom was holding. Then I recognized the bracelets and realized why my mom had given them to us.

She said, "I was hoping I wouldn't have to give you these after the last time you switched places, but I guess you need a reminder. I'll take them off when you both turn 12."

The bracelets were super tight. We didn't turn 12 for five more months. All we could say was, "Yes ma'am," and promised to never switch places again."

Mom warned, "You better not."

I wasn't going to be eating dinner that night either. I was sent straight to my room along with Zelena. I had gotten used to that, and to no dinner. As I looked over my homework, I realized it wasn't multiple-choice. Yay! That really cheered me up. I was to write an essay about a moment in my life. I wrote:

Once upon a time there was a girl named Zoey. She was beautiful, kind, sweet, nice, great, popular, awesome, smart, fun, amazing, thoughtful, talented, funny, gifted, and best of all, a great listener. One day Zoey had decided to switch places with her twin sister, Zelena, because Zelena was a little insecure about herself, and Zoey thought it would be a great opportunity for her sister to experience what it's like to be as awesome as her. So the next day, Zoey wore Zelena's shirt, which said "ZELENA", and Zelena wore Zoey's shirt, which said "ZOEY".

In second period, Zoey went to her sister's advanced biology class, while Zelena went to her sister's art class. In biology class they were dissecting frogs, and Zoey felt bad for the frog she was dissecting. Not because she was tearing it apart, but because it was a boring faded green color. Zoey didn't like faded green, but she did like faded jeans, especially the ones that were pre-ripped. One of her absolute favorite movie stars had a brand with an entire line of ripped jeans, and I...I mean Zoey had come across them in the mall one day and begged her mom to buy them. Her mom gave in, and Zoey even managed to get a shirt to match (from the same brand)! Everyone complimented her outfit when she wore it the next day, and her best friend, Sarah, even asked if Zoey would lend them to her for school the next Friday. Zoey, of course, being the generous, kind, and caring person she was, let Sarah borrow them. Sarah was a little insecure about herself, and honestly didn't have the best fashion sense, and even once wore the most hideous green pants to school, which reminds me, back to the frog dissecting.

Zoey felt bad for the frog for being boring green, then she saw a blue chemical near her, and an idea popped into her head! She put the dissected frog in the beaker that held the blue chemical stuff. The chemicals exploded, blasting color everywhere in the bland room! Everyone yelled so happy about what Zoey had just done. The teacher yelled the loudest of all, in fact, she sent her to the principal's office, so that Zoey could tell the principal the news in person.

Zoey made her way to the principal's office with a little bit of blue goo on her, but she didn't mind that much, she was just so happy that she had helped spread color to the world! When she reached the office her sister was there too, to celebrate Zoey and what she had done. Then the principal walked in, and she was surprised. She also had figured out that they had switched places, probably because only the unique, helpful, and creative Zoey could do something so great. She even gave Zoey and Zelena (because if Zelena hadn't agreed to switch places the splash of color would never happen) the rest of the school day off! And let them spend an hour in detention after school for a month, so they could keep the fun around even when school ended! Zoey was so thankful and generous that she volunteered to scrape all the gum off the desks in the entire school! After she scrapped some gum, her parents came and picked her and Zelena up. When they got home their mom gave them both beautiful matching bracelets!

The end!

I cheered up after writing my report and went to brush my teeth. I accidently squirt way too much toothpaste onto my toothbrush. Have you ever tried to put toothpaste back *into* the tube? It just wasn't happening. It got all over my hands before I got a nasty itch on my head, which I had to scratch. Toothpaste got all into my beautiful red hair. I had to take two showers to get it out. Let's just say it wasn't the best day ever, even though my essay was totally amazing.

2

The Audition

HE next day I sat next to Sarah and her friend Chloe on the bus. Chloe was always in the spotlight. She was a cheerleader, the lead in all school plays, and did glee club. She wasn't just super-talented. She was super-*pretty*. She had long blonde neat curls, blue eyes, and always wore trendy outfits.

That day Sarah told me about a play she wrote and would be directing. "I wrote a play called *Snow in Texas*, and I'll be directing it!" with excitement in her voice.

"And I'm auditioning for Chloe, of course. The part is literally made for me," Chloe said with pride.

"I'd like to audition for Chloe," I said, which probably shocked Chloe. "I was once a reindeer in my second grade Christmas play. By the way I got a new app that lets me swap faces with another person. I tried doing it with Zelena, but for some reason nothing happened."

"Okay, just come to the school auditorium tomorrow at eleven o'clock, and you can audition," Sarah said.

I was so excited. I had always wanted to star in a school play, and I finally had the chance. I wanted to be as prepared as possible, so at lunch I asked Sarah how I could prep for my audition.

"Well... the role of Chloe is supposed to be a blonde."

"Hmmm..." I responded and thought for a moment. "I guess I'll go to the hair salon after school to get my hair bleached. My mom works there, so I may get her employee discount. Wait. Even with the employee discount I don't have enough money. I don't have *any* money since I spent it all on art supplies. Oh well, I guess paintbrushes aren't cheap. Maybe I can try to bleach my hair by myself. Mom has bleach at home in her bathroom cabinet on the left. I saw it when I was looking for her makeup yesterday that I wasn't supposed to touch."

I rode the bus to my house where I was alone, the perfect chance to bleach my hair without anyone stopping me. Zelena was volunteering at "Help Houston Stay Clean". Zach was busy at a "Science Geeks" game fan club that he had organized (even though nobody was a member of the fan club beside himself). Both Mom and Dad were working.

I went into my Mom's bathroom and opened the left side of the cabinet's drawer (which I was forbidden to touch). I quickly grabbed the bleach in fear that someone would catch what I was doing at any second.

I was ready to put in the bleach. I had seen Mom do it at work with hair dye, so I knew how to apply it. My Mom usually did it over her bathroom sink, but I just used the kitchen sink. I had my head over the sink as I scrubbed in the bleach like shampoo. After I was done scrubbing it in, I poured yellow food coloring all over my head. I then turned on the kitchen sink's cold water to rinse. The water was a little cold, but I just thought about how elegant and sophisticated my new blonde locks would look, instead of silly and playful red hair. Along with Chloe's jaw drop when she would see what a perfect Chloe I would be in the play, and how she would probably get the role of a tree.

I turned off the freezing water and went into my bathroom to see my hair in the little mirror that I had to stand on my toes to see myself in. As soon as I saw myself I screamed at the top of my lungs. I had bright yellow hair! Like the sun! Or a lemon! I knew I shouldn't have used that bleach. It was bad enough being fire. I was now the sun!

Suddenly I heard footsteps! I cracked open the bathroom door to see who it could be. It was Zelena! I knew that goody-two-shoes would tell on me, even after eleven years of being twins. Maybe if I begged Zelena she wouldn't tell Mom or Dad, and I'd just wear a hat until I could somehow fix my hair. I walked into the living room where Zelena was starting on homework. As soon as she looked up, she couldn't believe her eyes.

"What happened to you?" she asked with concern.

I calmly said, "At least people can tell us apart easily now. Look Zelena, I know I wasn't supposed to do this and I'll never do it again, so please don't tell Mom and Dad. Please. Remember that time I didn't tell Mom and Dad that you accidently didn't dot an eye in one of your papers for school? And I can never keep secrets."

Zelena thought for a moment, and I thought she was about to agree to keep it a secret, but Zach walked in. He definitely couldn't keep it a secret. I was doomed.

"Woah!" Zach said. "You look like a sunflower! You look like you washed your hair in yellow paint! You look like a school bus! You look like you're in the middle of a red light and green light!"

I was humiliated by Zach's clever remarks, but my parents weren't home yet. I still had time to fix my hair or hide in a closet. Then Mom and Dad walked in!

"What did you do?!" Mom yelled.

"I bleached my hair blonde without asking you," I confessed. "I'm so sorry and I'll never do it again, so please fix my hair, please. Just send me to bed with no dinner."

Mom said, "I'm not fixing your hair 'till tomorrow. That's your punishment. Now go to bed!"

I understood going to bed with no dinner, but now I had to audition for the role of Chloe with bright yellow hair. I certainly would stand out compared to everybody else auditioning. I was totally doomed.

The next morning Mom was making pancakes, my favorite. After she finished organizing the ingredients, she got a call from work and had to leave early. Mom told us just to have cereal, but I would always rather have pancakes.

I decided to make them myself, since Mom had already organized the ingredients. *It couldn't be that hard, could it?* The first thing I did was taste test each ingredient to make sure they were all good. The first ingredient I tried was the flour. It had no taste, but Mom always put it in, so I put it in. The next was the vanilla. It smelled good. I expected it to taste good, but let's just say, it was awful. It was definitely not as great as it smelled. I certainly didn't want something that tasted so horrible in my pancakes, so I left out the vanilla. Next I tried a big spoonful of sugar. It was delicious, so I put in extra. I cracked an egg open and tried the yellow stuff inside of it. Yuck! But I still added two eggs. Next I tried the milk right from the carton. It was all right, but I thought chocolate milk would be better. I was pretty sure that was how you made chocolate pancakes, and I loved chocolate pancakes. I stirred everything together and put it on the griddle. I took the pancakes off after two minutes.

I shouted to Zelena and Zach, "Who wants pancakes?!"

They both responded by yelling, "Not me!"

I just said to myself, "more for me." I ate the whole giant pile of chocolate pancakes. Delicious! Even with the not so great flour and eggs.

When I was getting ready for the audition, I put my new yellow hair in a bun to try hiding it. I could still tell my hair was yellow, so I borrowed one of Zach's "Science Geeks" hats he had made for his "Science Geeks Game Fan Club". I still had a little bit of time, so I decided to practice. I thought my acting was fine, but Sarah had told me that the role of Chloe involved singing. I did the basic warm up of singing, "Do, Ray, Me, Fa, So, La, Te, Do". I thought I sang beautifully, but apparently my neighbor, Mr. Carson, had another opinion.

He yelled, "Stop singing!" from his front porch.

Mr. Carson was in his seventies, lived by himself, and was usually very nice, unlike when he told me to stop singing. Maybe living alone makes you cranky. I decided that I'd just practice while walking to school, assuming Mr. Carson didn't recognize good singing when he heard it.

It was amazing. I never knew I was such a great singer. A lady weeding her front yard said, "I've never heard a voice quite like yours". She shook her head and put on headphones when I passed her. Maybe she thought I was famous and was trying to find me on iTunes.

When I reached the school auditorium I saw Chloe in a white shirt that said **SHINE** in pink. She also wore a short pink ruffled skirt, a pair of sparkly white sandals, and matching headband in her beautiful curls. I wished her good luck.

Chloe turned around and said, "H.... oh, your hair."

I had forgotten about my yellow hair. It must have fallen out of the bun while on my way to the audition.

"Oh, I tried to bleach my hair blonde," I said. "I added yellow food coloring to make it more yellow, I added a tad too much. I know, it looks like a rubber ducky, but it's better than a fire hydrant. My Mom's going to fix it later. Do you know how bad vanilla tastes? Chocolate's way better. I've always wondered how brown hair would look on me, or maybe black hair. No, it would be too dark for my pale skin. I burn easily in the sun, and so does Zelena. Of course you would think that, because we are twins. Did you know some twins aren't identical? Some are even brother and sister. There is also such a thing as triplets, which are three kids! I don't want to have triplets! Too much work; I'd like to have three kids, but not all at the same time. Although I could name them Aly, Alice, and

Alyson if I had triplets and they were all girls."

Chloe simply said, "Interesting."

Girl after girl auditioned for the role of Chloe, but finally it was my turn. I delivered lines from a piece of paper I was given. "I wish snow would come to Texas. It would really make my Christmas special. I've never seen a flake of snow in my life. I would make a snowman, go ice skating, and more if it would snow."

I was also supposed to sing some silly song about snow, but why would someone just burst into song? Instead of singing, I told them how I felt. "I don't understand why someone would just sing songs that they make up as they go along in real life. I've never seen anyone ever do that. Although, I have heard Zach singing in the shower while I was outside the bathroom door. He takes forever in the shower, and-"

Sarah interrupted me by saying, "That's enough Zoey! We don't need to hear about how long or what your brother does in the shower. Next!"

I walked offstage disappointed. I had blown my one shot to be the lead in a school play. I had bleached my hair for nothing, and the part was probably going to be given to Chloe. The part was "literally made for her". Chloe gracefully walked onstage, said her lines dramatically without looking at the paper, and sang the silly song so well it didn't seem silly. Sarah stood up and applauded as if nobody else had auditioned. If only I had sung the song instead of wondering *why* I had to sing the song.

Sarah sat back down and said, "Thank you all for auditioning. I'll post the cast list on the bulletin board tomorrow after school."

Mom picked me up in our nasty brown van to take me to the hair salon. I sat in the swivel chair and took off Zach's hat that I had borrowed. Everyone stared at me and a few whispered to each other about my bright yellow mane.

"So, how are you going to fix my hair?" I politely asked. "I want it to be just like before, but maybe a little less red. I've learned my lesson. Yellow is not my color. My audition was awful. I won't get the part of Chloe, but I'm a great singer. I could work on the streets playing for pennies like that guy we saw outside of the gas station yesterday. He was awful, so I'd get paid a lot more than him. I want spaghetti for dinner tonight. I made chocolate pancakes this morning when you left for work. They were delicious. You should have been there to try them. So how are you going to fix my hair?"

Mom said, "Well I'm going to have to dye it back to your red."

"Please don't, Mom! There has to be another way, but if

you could dye it less red that would be great. What if you dyed my hair gray, like Grandpa, Grandma, and Mr. Carson's hair? The weird thing is I've never seen a kid with gray hair before. I guess only adults get it. Besides I'd look silly with gray hair, won't I?"

"First of all, your hair will be fine if I dye it back," Mom said. "Second of all, I'm not dying it less red. That's part of your punishment. Third of all, you shouldn't worry about gray hairs because you've given me enough of those."

After Mom dyed my hair, it did look just like before, red as a tomato. Even though I didn't get my hair dyed less red, it was a lot better than yellow. I would never bleach my hair again.

*
* *

The next day Sarah posted the cast of *Snow in Texas* on the school's bulletin board as promised. Everyone huddled up around the board except Chloe and me. There was no use in looking. I knew I wouldn't get the part, but I didn't know why Chloe didn't look. Did she have doubts about her getting the part, or was she so sure she was going to get it that she wasn't even going to check?

I asked her, "Why aren't you going to see the cast? I'm sure you got the lead, as always. By the way, I got my hair fixed. It's just like it was before I bleached it. I don't like my parents' old brown van. It has a moldy chicken nugget that I squashed in the cup holder when I was four. Trust me, you do not want to ride in it.

Chloe said, "Well, to answer the first topic you discussed, I didn't get the role of Chloe. Sarah decided she wanted the role all to herself. I am the angel named Joy. She's the most important character in the play."

I was glad Chloe didn't get the part, and happy for Sarah. She deserved the lead after working so hard on the play. By the way the angel named Joy only had two lines. So Chloe was lying.

Later at dinner, my parents had some news to share. I wasn't sure if it was going to be good news. Sometimes news is about me. Most of the time when news is about me, it is bad news. But sometimes news is good, like when we decided to get our Labradoodle Zane, or when we found out Zelena was the top student out of our entire fifth grade class back in elementary school.

My parents had not announced the news, and it was almost time for dinner to be over. I was on phase four in my meal, the last phase. In phase four I eat my roll, because my mom always insists that I not eat my roll until last. I tried to eat my roll as slowly as I could, because I really hoped my parents would announce the news before phase four was over.

I couldn't take it any longer. I stuffed the rest of my roll in my mouth and yelled, "Tell us the news already!"

Mom and Dad exchanged looks for a minute, and then finally Dad said, "Sorry, we thought it'd be best to tell you after everyone was done eating."

"But since you're so eager to know," said Mom, "I suppose it wouldn't hurt to tell you now. Well, here's the news."

I suddenly felt my roll stick to my throat. I couldn't get it out! It was lodged in my throat! I couldn't breathe! I started gagging, and Mom ran towards me to perform the Heimlich maneuver. She thrust her arms into my stomach, and the roll came flying out, which was a relief to me. As the roll flew out of my mouth, Zane, who was lying next to Zelena's seat, jumped right up in the air and caught it! Zach and Zelena burst into laughter. Mom and Dad didn't exactly see the humor in it, so they ordered all of us to do our homework without learning the news. *Really?*

3

Christmas in Colorado

MY parents told us the news the morning after the Heimlich maneuver drama with my roll. We were going to spend Christmas in Colorado with my grandparents. Several weeks later, we were on the plane getting ready to take off. I still wasn't sure if it was good news or bad news. I loved seeing my grandparents, and I loved the idea of spending Christmas with them, but I wasn't so sure that I loved the idea of not spending Christmas at home. I loved spending Christmas at home with Zane, and seeing him try to open his stocking, and I loved baking cookies, and giving them to all the neighbors on Christmas day, but I was also excited to go skiing and see the snow in Colorado.

Instead of trying to decide if Christmas would be better in Colorado, I tried to relax and enjoy the flight. I couldn't wait to know what it feels like to soar through the sky. I had never been on a plane and neither had Zelena, but we both had different reactions to this new experience. Zelena was holding onto the armrests tightly with her knees up to her chest tightly and her eyes shut tightly. I shouted "Wee!" with my hands up as the plane flew up into the clouds.

After the plane had taken off, it was kind of boring. Zelena had settled down and was reading, Zach was playing "Science Geeks" on his phone, and Mom and Dad were watching a movie on the screen. Finally, something happened. A young flight attendant with short brown hair and green eyes came over with a cart that had snacks and beverages.

The lady said, "Hello, would you like some pretzels, peanuts, or a beverage?"

"My name's Zoey Grace Song," I said, happy that I had someone to talk to. "But you can call me Zoey, that's Zoey Z-O-E-Y. Don't forget the Y. Nice to meet you; it must be fun to travel all around the world."

The flight attendant said, "Well actually, this is my first-"

I said, "Tell me about yourself! Actually you don't have to if you don't want to. I'll just tell you about my life."

"Oh, I'm fine, you don't have to-"

"Well where should I get started? I know, my first memory. It happened when I was four years, three months, one week, eight minutes, and 15 seconds old..."

I kept telling the lady about my life, and before I knew

it we were in Colorado, and I was still telling her about my 3rd memory. I really thought the flight attendant liked me. She even gave me special permission to get off the plane first and carried my carry-ons.

After we got our luggage, a cab took us to my Grandparent's cabin. We went up a mountain that was covered with snow, and next to several other cabins was my Grandparent's cabin. It was made of giant wooden logs, had a dark green roof, chimney, and a front porch with two rocking chairs.

It was late and we all were tired, except me; I was ready to go skiing. Mom forced me to go to bed, but even if I had been tired, I wouldn't have wanted to go to bed. Mine was a bunk bed with three beds on it that I would share with Zach and Zelena in the loft upstairs. I have a fear of bunk beds! I believe that if you sleep on the top bunk, you might fall off, and if you sleep on the bottom bunk, the top bunk might fall on you. I got stuck with the very bottom bunk, so I had to worry about two bunks falling on me. It was a restless night until I finally went to sleep at two o'clock in the morning.

The next day we were supposed to go skiing, so Mom put me in layer over layer of clothes. I asked her if it was really necessary, and Mom said yes. I didn't know why, so I took off a few layers when she wasn't watching. I stepped outside into the freezing ice-cold snow and wished I had those layers. When Mom walked to the front porch, I was nearly frozen.

"I'm cold! Why... didn't... you tell me it was going to be so.... c... cold out here? I can hardly speak because I'm shivering!" I complained.

"What happened to those jackets and coats I put you in?" Mom asked.

"I took them o.. off," I said with chattering teeth.

I put my coats and jackets back on and snuggled in the warmth.

We took Grandpa's car to the slopes. Zach, Zelena, Mom, Dad, and I were on the bunny slope, or were *supposed* to be. There were four slopes: the bunny slope, the green slope, the blue slope, and the black diamond slope. Now, I liked the idea of chasing bunnies, the color green, and the color blue, but I wanted to chase diamonds! The rest of the family could chase bunnies, but I wanted to chase diamonds. When no one was looking, not even my grandparents who came to watch us, I snuck away to the diamond lift, which led to the diamond slope.

When it was time to get off the lift, I said to the lift master, "Excuse me, but where are the diamonds?"

The lift master pointed to a slope ahead of me and replied, "Those are the diamonds right there."

I hopped on the last lift, which went way up high in the sky. I skied down the slope and it felt incredible. For two seconds. Then somehow I tumbled down the slope and felt a huge amount of pain in my left leg. I screamed and cried and then two men in orange vests came and carried me down the mountain on a sled.

I managed to say through the pain, "Are you taking me to the diamonds?"

After the men were finished hauling me down, they put me in an ambulance that headed to the nearest emergency room, and I spent the night there. They gave me a white cast for my leg and crutches. My parents were mad that I went on the diamond slope without asking. They were even angrier than the time I got my tongue stuck to the flagpole at school.

Mom and Zelena didn't go skiing on my behalf the day after I broke my leg, or maybe they didn't want to break their legs either. Grandma and Grandpa didn't go watch Zach and Dad ski either. Zelena and I watched a movie inside about a famous ice skater, which made me think about my broken leg the whole time. When Zach and Dad came back from the slopes, Zach rubbed it in my face and Zelena's face that he had moved on to the green slope, but Dad said Zach had fallen flat on his face.

Finally after a long week of just sitting around, it was Christmas Eve. I had presents for everyone. I got Zelena a locket and me a locket. They were both half of a heart and if you put them together they say TWINS. I wrote my Mom a five-paged poem and got her perfume. I got Dad four passes to go on a date night with Mom. I got Zach a "Science Geeks" cheat book (maybe it would help him score more than one point). I bought Grandma yarn for her knitting, and I drew Grandpa a picture of us together and framed it.

There was nothing to do on crutches. Zach and Dad were on the slopes skiing, and Grandpa was trying to call people on his new phone while Grandma, Mom, and Zelena knitted. I couldn't ski, it was impossible to teach Grandpa to use a phone, and I was terrible at knitting. I decided to use some paints and paper to paint zebras. That always entertained me. Then I looked at a plain glass ornament on the Christmas tree in the living room, where I was painting. The ornament was so colorless and had nothing special about it. Suddenly, an idea popped into my head. I'd make the ornament special by painting a zebra on it. So I grabbed the ornament on the tree from the desk where I was sitting, because I couldn't stand up to get it. The tree wobbled a little when I grabbed the ornament but didn't fall over. I started to paint the best zebra I could on the ornament, and I was just about to put it back on the tree when Mom and Grandma walked in and saw me.

"Zoey Grace Song!" Mom yelled.

"Don't you like it?" I asked Mom, wondering if that was why she yelled. "I painted the best zebra I could. The ornament was so plain before. I thought this would add a splash of color, not the type of splash of color as the time I dyed my hair yellow, but you know, the good kind. This is the good kind of splash of color, right?"

Mom exclaimed, "No! It's not the good kind! That ornament is one hundred years old!"

Then Grandma said, "Oh, it's fine Zoey. In fact, I think that zebra makes the ornament special."

That night, Zelena helped make Christmas Eve dinner with Mom and Grandma. I wanted to help, but Mom told me that it was best if I stayed out of the kitchen. Even though I didn't help, Christmas Eve dinner was good, and after dinner we put out cookies for Santa and carrots for his reindeer. Mom made us go to bed early, because if we didn't Mom said Santa wouldn't come. I had overcome my fear of bunk beds, so I was able to go right to sleep.

I woke up the next morning at five o'clock. It was Christmas day! I couldn't wait to open gifts! But I couldn't do it yet, because everyone was asleep. My whole family (including my grandparents) likes to sleep late. I tried falling back asleep like Mom always tells me to do when I wake up early, but I couldn't go back to sleep at all. *If only I could wake them up*, I thought. Wait. *I could.*

I yelled, "Get up! Get up! Get up!" To Zelena and Zach.

Mom, Dad, Grandpa, and Grandma ran into my room with sleepy eyes. Apparently I had, indeed, woken everyone up.

I asked, "So since we're all up now, who wants to open presents? I want to open mine first; don't you all love Christmas. Especially this year because now you all know the joy of getting up at five o'clock."

Mom and Dad made me sleep in their bed, and told me not to wake them up. I just lay there, thinking of all the presents I'd get three hours later when everyone would wake up.

When I received permission to get out of bed, I walked as fast as I could with my crutches into the living room to open gifts. "Me first! Me first!" I yelled.

The first gift I opened was from Zach. It was his old "Science Geeks" shirt that no longer fit him, (thanks a lot Zach.) Then I opened Zelena's present to me, which was a scarf, or a hat, I couldn't tell, but she had knit it for me. The next gift I opened was from Grandma and Grandpa. It was a zebra stuffed animal, the perfect wife for Mr. Stripes who was my other zebra stuffed animal. Then I opened Mom and Dad's gift. It was in a small box and didn't look like much. But when I opened it I saw a sparkly diamond necklace. They must have gotten it from the diamond slope. I also got a how-to-draw book from Santa and candy in my stocking.

At the end of our trip, we took a cab to the airport. I saw the same flight attendant from the ride to Colorado, but for some reason she ran away in the middle of serving snacks. I was disappointed that I didn't get to talk to her, but got to have a good long conversation with myself. When the flight was over, I saw the flight attendant hiding in the front of the plane.

I said, "There you are! What are you doing hiding over there, flight attendant, whatever your name is? I should learn your name. Wait, let me guess. Is it Jane, or Julie, or Betty? I bet it's Betty. Well Betty, we have a lot of catching up to do. Like my broken leg; I also never got to finish telling you my third memory. Let's see, where did I leave off? Oh, right. One day long, long ago, it was ninety-two degrees outside-"

Then Betty the flight attendant yelled, "Security!"

Two strong men in uniforms came and one carried me off the plane; the other carried my carry on and crutches.

When we got home, Mr. Carson was supposed to bring Zane back home, because he had taken care of him when we were away. When Mr. Carson came, he didn't only bring Zane; he also brought a golden doodle that was a puppy. I knew the puppy wasn't Mr. Carson's but didn't know whose it was.

I asked, "Whose puppy is that? It's cute. Oh, and I broke my leg while chasing diamonds and I got a diamond necklace for Christmas. You can sign my cast! I'm also going to have Sarah and all my friends sign it. I'm going to have them sign it with a pink pen I'll carry around with me everywhere. Although I may use a light blue pen instead, or maybe I'll carry around both, or every color except black, brown, gray, white, and green. Black, brown, and gray are all too dark; white's too plain, and green's too ugly. Although bright green grass is nice, but I don't like green clothes, except the dark green sweeter Grandma knitted me."

Dad said, "Surprise! We got you all a puppy!"

"It's a golden doodle and it's a girl," Mom said.

"Really?" I said. "So it, I mean she can have puppies someday? Let's name her Betty, like the flight attendant on the plane, or Zuri. Thank you for the puppy; I'll bring her to Chloe's house and brag about her. Chloe has always wanted a dog and now I have two, while she doesn't even have one. She also doesn't have a broken leg, but it's not really a good thing to have a broken leg."

We ended up naming her Noodle, as in Noodle the golden doodle. Even though I suffered a broken leg, it was one of the best Christmases ever.

4

The Babysitters

IT was a struggle to get around with crutches at school. Luckily, people helped me carry my books to class and open my locker. The only good thing about my broken leg was people could easily tell Zelena and me apart. After our first day back at school, Mom and Dad had an announcement that they wanted to share with us.

Dad said, "Your Mom and I have decided to use one of your date night passes, Zoey. We are going out tomorrow but your usual babysitter, Mrs. Seller, is sick. So we've decided to let Zach babysit you both."

"You both!" I said, "As in me and Zelena? Zach is the least responsible person ever! All he ever does is play that 'Science Geeks' game. How could you allow him to take care of your precious little angels?"

I absolutely did not want to have him babysit me. *Actually*, I thought to myself, *this could be a good thing*. I could do whatever I wanted, because Zach wouldn't care. So when Mom asked again if we were okay with this arrangement, I said,

"Yes ma'am."

The next day I came home from a long day at school; I just wanted to sit down and relax. I had a seventy-five multiple-choice question ELA test on a book we had read. Three of my least favorite things: books, tests, and multiple-choice. I was also hungry, so I grabbed a chocolate bar from the pantry and sat down on the worn out, beige couch in the living room. I started to do my homework while gorging the chocolate bar but got distracted by Noodle. Noodle was sitting right in front of me, tilting her head slightly to the right, with big brown sad puppy eyes that were watching me gorge my chocolate bar. I tried to stay strong and focus on my homework but gave in and let Noodle eat the remaining half of my chocolate bar.

Before Mom and Dad left to go on their date at a sophisticated and fancy restaurant that had no kids' menus, they gave Zach some rules. Rule number one: no friends allowed, (but he didn't even have friends). Rule number two: make Zelena and me go to bed at nine o' clock, no later. Rule number three: no fires, explosions, floods, dying hair, dissecting frogs, or broken bones.

"Good night, have a good time, I know I will with my brother that I love, babysitting me. We're going to have so much fun tonight! We'll do makeovers, which Zach really needs, and Zach will sing us a lovely lullaby, won't you Zach, oh, of course you will. Anyway, I love you and have an exquisite night. I know I will," I said acting as angelic and innocent as I could while thinking about going into my parent's bathroom and using my Mom's makeup, which I wasn't supposed to even touch.

Mom said, "Good night sweethearts! Take good care of them Zach!"

"I will," he said.

As soon as my parents left, Zach lazily plopped onto the couch and started to text someone on his phone. I couldn't imagine what poor person was so unpopular that he had no choice but to be friends with my brother.

I said, "Who are you texting? I can't imagine how lonely they are. Let's invite whoever you are texting to dinner sometime, but not tonight, because of rule number one. By the way, what are we having for dinner; I'm starving; do you even know how to cook? Don't worry. I could whip up some pancakes. Wait, we're out of eggs. I guess Zelena could cook something; she's great at housework; except knitting. My scarf or whatever it was turned out terrible, but it's the thought that counts. She had spent weeks working on it. Grandma's a great knitter; she can even sew; she once made me a cute yellow dress with polka dots when I was four; it was a while ago when that happened, but it was my favorite dress, and now it's my favorite shirt. I didn't want to sell it to the thrift store last year, so now it's a shirt, but now it's more like a crop top, but crop tops are in style now."

Zach ignored me and put on his ear buds as if I were invisible. I assumed he didn't want to be bothered by me, so I thought of which fun thing I'd do first. I decided on using Mom's makeup. I just wanted to try a little bit of her light pink glossy lipstick, but a little bit turned into a lot, and just lipstick turned into mascara, blue eye shadow, blush, and eyeliner. I thought, the more makeup the prettier I'd look. I even tried to curl my hair, but after I curled it, my hair started to stick up.

Suddenly, while I was still in my parents' bathroom, I heard rap music blasting through the house and a crowd of people talking. I walked into the living room as fast as I could with my crutches. If Zach had invited people over, he was in trouble. When I got to the living room, Zach had not only invited people over, he had thrown a party! There was red soda spilled on the white carpet that would stain it forever; Mom's antique glass lamp with flower print on it lay in pieces on the floor, and there were girls with way too short dresses!

I walked up to Zach in the middle of the crowd of people dancing to rap music. I yelled to him over the crowd and music, "What's going on Zach?! Who are all of these popular and cool people?! Mom and Dad said 'No friends over'!"

Zach pushed through the crowd. I followed him and accidently ran into some big and strong guy and fell because of my broken leg. I quickly picked up my crutches and found Zach in the kitchen.

I said, "Now that there isn't a bunch of noise, who are those people? You're going to be in a lot of trouble with Mom and Dad. I can't imagine what kind of punishment you'll get in for disobeying them, breaking a lamp, staining the carpet, and having girls over with really short dresses!"

Zach said, "Okay first of all, I didn't stain the carpet or break the lamp. Matthew Owens, the most popular guy in school, and his friends did it. He just wanted to have a party and when he heard our parents would not be home tonight, he asked to throw it at my place. I agreed, but I didn't know things would get out of hand like this. Plus everyone's making fun of me in there! Please don't tell Mom and Dad that I threw this party, I'll end the party early and clean up afterwards."

I said, "Fine. I won't tell them, but you know I'm not good at keeping secrets. Remember that time I told on you for not putting on sunscreen while you went and got the mail. That day I also got a clothing catalog. It had a cute white ruffled tank top for only ten dollars in it and it was on sale for twenty percent off! Although I didn't buy it, because shipping and handling cost twenty dollars, and the shirt was all the way from England; I want to go to England someday; I hear the steering wheels on cars are on the other side there!"

"Thanks, Zoey. By the way, you look like a clown with

that makeup and your hair like that."

When Zach and I walked back into the crowded living room a football player threw a football and hit a window, Noodle threw up the chocolate bar I had fed her, and someone spilled ranch dip on the coffee table! As all of this was happening, Mom and Dad came home.

Dad was furious. Mom was speechless. He said, "Everyone! GO!"

All the guests ran out and Zach turned off the rap music.

Zach said, "Why are you home early?"

"Zelena called us. You are grounded for a month, Zach. That means no 'Science Geeks.' Zoey, looks like you've been into my makeup, that I constantly have been telling you not to touch. Not only have you gotten into my makeup, but it also seems like you got into my curling iron! You're grounded for a week. No going anywhere. No friends over. No drawing. No phone. Now go to bed Zoey! We have to have a serious discussion with Zach."

"Yes ma'am," I cowered and left for my bedroom.

Zelena was already in bed, even though it was two hours before her bedtime. She always seemed to be the good girl, never getting into trouble. She must have a boring life, I thought.

Mom and Dad took my phone, art drawing pad and paints away. This was a way worse punishment than detention or being sent to bed with no dinner. I really shouldn't have gotten into Mom's makeup. She had warned me time after time not to do it.

Poor Zach. Mr. goody-two-shoes had really gotten himself in trouble. Trying to fit in didn't work out the way he had expected. I kind of felt bad for Zach. All he had wanted was to fit in. Like me.

My parents decided to go to the fancy restaurant the next night and choose another babysitter to watch us. They decided on my cousin, Carly, who was 19. She always wore her blonde hair in a neat bun, had freckles, which added a silliness to her serious face, and was *extremely* responsible. She was in her freshman year of college and was studying to be a doctor, which is a big deal. I knew Zelena would grow up to be just like her.

When Carly came that night she entered with her usual frown. It made her look older than she really was. She wasn't ever much fun. I expected that night to be boring. She would probably make us do chores or homework against our will. Mom walked up to Carly and was about to hug her. Carly just shook hands.

"A handshake shall do fine," Carly said. "Have a nice evening. I am aware of Zoey and Zach's punishments, so please do not fret over me forgetting. I shall keep them under control and make sure they cause no mischief. I shall also make sure they go to sleep at their bedtimes." She was very professional, like she had been planning this for years instead of hours.

Mom said, "Well, I was about to tell you the rules, but it seems like you have everything under control."

"Have a good evening, Uncle David and Aunt Linda."

"Bye Mom and Dad," Zelena and I said in unison.

"Goodnight," they said before leaving.

"Hello children." Carly touched up her bun. "I assume you've all completed your chores assigned for the day."

"Yes ma'am," Zelena, Zach, and I said.

"Well, I will work on my studies while you dust the living room, Zoey. It's awfully dusty, and I remember from my last visit that you're in charge of dusting. Zelena and Zach occupy yourselves among this educational documentary about animals."

"Yes ma'am," we all said.

"Well then, sounds like we have our evening planned," Carly sighed.

Zelena and Zach watched the animal documentary while I dusted. I knew something like that would happen; she made me do a chore and my poor siblings watch a boring movie. After I was finished, my stomach growled. I was hungry.

I walked up to Carly, who was studying and said, "I'm finished dusting. Can we have dinner? I'm starving. I didn't eat a big lunch like I normally do; because I knew I'd probably not get in trouble for doing something and be sent to bed with no dinner. I'm trying to be on my best behavior, because I'm already punished. I no longer have my art supplies or phone, which you already know. I'm bored without them now."

"Hmmm. I'll go make dinner and you can help me," Carly kindly said, with a smile on her face that made her look more youthful.

I wasn't sure if cooking with strict and responsible Carly would be fun, but something about the look on her face made her seem like there was more to her. We waked into the kitchen and I suggested making my famous pancakes for dinner, but Carly had other plans.

"Actually, I'm working on a new recipe." she said with the same smile. "Now first let's wash our hands."

I washed my hands as Carly did the same.

"Next, let's get you a special apron. I brought one with

me. It's right here in my bag." Carly gave me an apron with lots of ruffles, pink, and polka dots.

"Thank you so much; it's beautiful. Did you make it? It's so creative and unique. You most also love pink. I love it too! I can't wait to find out what we're cooking. I'm starving. All I had for lunch was three chocolate chip cookies, a peanut butter and jelly sandwich, and two bags of potato chips."

"Well, I didn't make this, but my Mom did when I was your age. I did design it though, and now it's yours. Anyway, we're cooking my famous macaroni and cheese, extra cheesy."

"Yum!" I said. "Thanks for the apron; hopefully I won't get cheese on it. Let's get started; how about you get the ingredients out and I'll start shredding the cheese; maybe I'll also tell you about me; I have lots to tell you.

I started shredding cheese and sneaking a few shreds of cheeses to eat, while telling Carly about how I broke my leg.

Carly laughed after my story and said, "What a funny story."

There was more to Carly. I never would have thought responsible Carly would laugh at one of my stories. I wanted to know more about this Carly. She spoke about her love of cooking a lot. She made the cheese sauce perfectly and cooked the macaroni perfectly. We then watched it bake in the oven.

"So, how's learning how to be a doctor going? I've always wanted to be an artist; I love drawing; I'd like to show you some of my artwork but I'm punished; I got punished for putting on my Mom's makeup and using her curling iron. Zach said I looked like a clown after I put on the makeup."

Carly said, "Learning to be a doctor is going well. I'm top in my class."

"Really, it must be fun if you're top in your class. Zelena's top in every class she takes; I'm only top in my art class; I don't think Mrs. Lewis, my ELA teacher, likes me that much. She always says, 'You', very harshly when I enter her classroom."

"Well actually, learning how to be a doctor isn't really fun. I would much rather be a chef, and maybe even open a restaurant."

"Then why are you going to be a doctor when you can be a chef? Being a chef sounds a lot more fun, and you're really good at it. I snuck a bite of the mac and cheese before you put it in the oven. It was way better than microwave mac and cheese."

"Well the pay's good, and my parents think a doctor's a great job. I've also never mentioned being a chef before."

"What about what you think? I mean, it is your life; doesn't your opinion matter? Maybe if you just tell them about your dream, they'll support you. My parents support me in my dream of being an artist."

Carly said, "I don't think they will; they think being a doctor's my dream. Well, the macaroni and cheese is done cooking. Do you want to try some fully cooked?"

I tried some and it was so rich and creamy. Carly would make a great chef, but a doctor was what she was going to be, sadly.

"So how do you get it so creamy? If you're still working on it like you say you are, stop working on it; it's perfect; this would taste great in a restaurant; maybe a restaurant called, I don't know, 'Carly's Café'. I can just see it on a big sign in pink towering above New York. It would have all the chefs and waiters wearing pink aprons just like mine. You would be head of it all, but you know, just a thought."

"It's a nice thought, but it probably will never happen." Carly sounded a little sad. Then she cheered up. "Well, you know what makes the mac and cheese so creamy? It's a secret ingredient, and you have to promise to never tell it to anyone."

"I'm not that good at keeping secrets, but when they're special I always keep them. Like the time my best friend Sarah told me about her secret of, oh forgot, I promised not to tell. That's happened like five times since she told me, but I always make sure I never tell it. This secret sounds special, so I promise not to tell it to anyone, ever!"

"Okay," Carly said then whispered the secret in my ear. "It's just what you would think would make it creamy. Cream."

I said, "Really? What a great idea. You know, I have a secret ingredient for my chocolate pancakes. Chocolate milk! I love chocolate; maybe next time you babysit, we can make them. Zelena can help too; she's great at housework, but she's never tried cooking; she also is not the greatest knitter, and she can't know my secret ingredient."

"Speaking of Zelena, she's probably still watching that boring movie with Zach. I'll call them to dinner. Zelena! Zach!" Carly said.

Zelena and Zach walked into the kitchen, smelling the creamy mac and cheese.

Zach said, "Hey, what smells so good?"

I answered proudly, "Super delicious mac and cheese that I helped make. Carly's been working on the recipe for it. The recipe is brilliant, and I don't think that anyone's mac and cheese is better."

"It's super creamy," Carly said then winked at me.

"You helped, Zoey? I'm surprised the kitchen didn't burn down!" Zach laughed as hard as he snorted.

"Well I'm sure she did a fantastic job," Zelena said, which made me wonder why Zelena stood up for me.

Carly served us each a big plate full of her mac and cheese.

Zach took a bite then said, "Wow, this is actually pretty good. What's in it?"

"Something special," I said then winked at Carly.

Carly and I had a special bond now. The night turned out completely different from what I had expected. I wondered if Carly would ever decide to tell her parents about her dreams of being a chef. Something told me she would. Someday.

5

The New Girl

ONE Monday morning I was on the bus sitting next to Sarah and Chloe. As usual, Chloe was bragging about some big achievement. Sarah had been spending quite a bit of time with Chloe, and I had just been tagging along. Sarah and I were still friends, but not best friends. Now it was all about popular and pretty Chloe.

After I zoned out in the middle of Chloe telling us about her getting to sing a whole song by herself in glee club, I noticed a girl I had never seen before getting on the bus. She had orange-red medium length wavy hair, brown eyes, and was short. She sat in the front of the bus by herself, looking out the window. I felt bad for the girl and wanted to get to know her. She seemed interesting. I had never had a friend before with red hair (besides Zelena). I hoped I would have her in one of my classes.

When I got to school, the girl from the bus was checking out her locker, which was right next to mine. I was thrilled to have her as my locker neighbor!

I said, "Hi, I'm Zoey Song. I like cooking, art, and having fun. Having fun is... well, fun! But it gets me in trouble sometimes. Like when I switched places with Zelena and went to her advanced chemistry class. We dissected frogs, and I put the frog skin in a blue chemical. Then the chemical blew up and got all over the classroom. I had detention for weeks, and I don't like being by myself and not talking."

"OK," The girl said, a little confused, then walked away.

"Maybe she's shy," I told myself. I was sure she'd like me once she got to know me. I hoped she'd get to know me better in a class, but she wasn't in my ELA class. I thought maybe I'd get to sit next to her at lunch, or I'd be able to talk to her at the lockers.

The next class was art, my favorite class that I looked forward to every day. It was taught by the best teacher ever! Ms. Crystal. She always complemented each student and hung every single one of our artwork pieces in the classroom. After only a year of her being our art teacher, the walls were completely covered with artwork.

When I walked into the art classroom, I was shocked. I saw the girl. She was sitting at the farthest table from the teacher, all by herself. I walked over and sat next to her. I smiled at her. She smiled back a small, weak smile, like she was scared.

Ms. Crystal delivered her usual warm and welcoming greeting. "Hello, class. I hope you all had a nice weekend. Today we have a new student, who we are thrilled to have. Her name's Maddie, and she just moved here *all* the way from New York. I thought it would be nice for us to get to know her better, so I was wondering, Maddie, if you'd like to come up here and tell us a little about yourself."

"Yes ma'am," said the girl from the bus (who must have been Maddie). She slowly walked to the front of the class. "Well, I like to draw and do gymnastics. I'm pretty good at drawing, but once I drew on the walls when I was eight, and my Mom wasn't happy."

"Thank you, Maddie, you can take your seat now," Ms. Crystal said.

Maddie went back to her seat next to me. I was glad that I got to know more about her and that she had a mischievous side.

Ms. Crystal said, "OK class, today we are going to paint animals. Now there are already paints, paintbrushes, and paper on each table. You all can start, and have fun painting."

I said, "Hi, I'm Zoey. You may remember me from the lockers. Welcome to Texas. It must be a lot different from New York. New York must have giant skyscrapers, famous people, and it someday will have Carly's Cafe. Carly's Cafe is a restaurant that my cousin Carly is going to open there someday. Although she's in college learning to be a doctor right now, someday she'll become a chef. I want to be an artist someday; I might draw zebras only; I love drawing zebras; I'm going to draw one right now. What animal are you going to draw?"

"I like zebras too. I'll also draw one," Maddie said.

After we both finished our paintings we showed each other our zebras. Maddie's was a lot better; hers perfectly captured the Zebra's form, and its black stripes were perfect, which made mine look like a weird looking horse, but she still told me mine looked good.

"Thanks," I said, "But yours is better. Hey, maybe we can draw at my house after school. Maybe you can even sleep over if it's OK with your parents. I can even cook dinner; I cook the best chocolate pancakes ever; you can help me make them; you'll love them, even though Zelena, Zach, and my parents don't even want to try them."

"OK. I guess I'll ask my parents if I can stay at your house tonight. I'll text them at lunch and tell you if they say yes, and I'll get my stuff after school."

"Great! This is going to be so much fun, and Zelena won't be home tonight. She's doing a fundraiser for 'Help Houston Stay Clean' tomorrow and is staying at a friend's house. So you can take Zelena's bed. By the way, Zelena's my twin. You can tell us apart now, because of my broken leg."

I told Maddie more about myself during the rest of art class. She also told me that back in New York she opened a lemonade stand with her best friend, Isabelle. Later at lunch she was sitting by herself again, so I sat next to her instead of Sarah, who was sitting next to Chloe, who was still talking about getting to sing that solo.

I asked Maddie, "So, did your parents say you could sleep at my house? I've already asked my parents; they said they'd love to have you spend the night. I'm sure Zach my older brother, Zane my dog, and Noodle my other dog, will also love to have you over. You're going to love Noodle; she's so fun and cute. You'll also love Zane; he's so lovable and sweet. You may not love Zach though, but you won't see much of him. He usually is playing some game called 'Science Geeks', but he's nice. Although he teases me, but that's just because he's my brother."

Maddie said, "Well, my parents said I could sleep over at your house. I'll get my things packed for tonight, and then I'll go straight to your house. My parents just want to know where your house is."

"Um, I live in a neighborhood called 'Glen Cove'. I don't know the address, but my house is one story, is painted light blue, and has a black roof. We want to paint it, but my parents say we can't waste money on painting the house. But I think the house would look a lot better. I like the color blue, and it might look good on a house, but not with a black roof. Black is supposed to go with everything, but I don't think it goes well with blue. I do like a blue dress with black polka dots that Zelena has, though. I've borrowed it ten times since she bought it a week ago."

Maddie said, "Really? I live in Glen Cove. Actually, I think I remember seeing your house. I live two streets over. Maybe we'll get to hang out more often now if we live in the same neighborhood."

I was glad that we lived close to each other, because none of my friends lived in Glen Clove. So now I'd finally have someone near me. I was so excited for that afternoon; I even made sure I behaved extra good at all of my classes so I wouldn't get detention. I didn't even raise my hand a single time in class, except once to answer a question in my social studies class, but I just told Mr. Peters that my hand fell asleep.

When I got home Zelena got her bags for her sleepover and left. I paced around the house, told my zebra stuffed animals about Maddie, and prepared the ingredients for my special chocolate pancakes within fifteen minutes of Maddie's arrival.

Maddie finally came with her Mom who looked just like her. She had short wavy orange-red hair, the same brown eyes, and was wearing a short black dress.

I said, "Hi Maddie and Maddie's Mom, I'm Zoey. Maddie and I have art class together. Maddie's a great artist, oh, and I want to ask you something. Did you ever get Maddie's drawing off the wall, and if you say no, I have another question. How did you sell your house with a drawing on the wall? My parents sold their starter home with a minor leakage problem, and the master bathroom had carpet, but the people who bought it were looking for a fixer upper house."

Maddie's mom replied in a fancy sophisticated tone, "Call me Mrs. Jones. It is a pleasure to meet the Zoey that has been influencing my dear Maddie. She has told me *quite* a bit about you. May I please meet your mother? I do not want to drop my dear Maddie off at some friend from school's house, who she's known for less than twenty-four hours, without even meeting her mother. Oh, children these days."

"Sure, Mrs. Jones," I said before shouting, "MOM! This lady wants to meet you!" I turned back to my new friend's mother. "Anyway, Mrs. Jones, it's good to meet you too. I love your dress; I wish I had a dress like yours; I also love your red nails; although I prefer hot pink, but whatever you like. I mean, I don't like Brussels sprouts, but Zelena loves them. You know my Dad used to feed Brussels sprouts to me like an airplane, but I never ate them. Speaking of airplanes, I once flew on a plane to Colorado. On the flight there was a flight attendant named Betty, I think."

Mom entered in a robe and slippers with a towel on her head. She had no makeup on either.

"Zoey, did you call me? I was in the shower." Then she saw Mrs. Jones and Maddie. "Oh, company. You two must be Maddie's Mom and Maddie. Hi, I'm Zoey's Mom, Linda."

"I can certainly see that you are both related by your indistinguishable temperaments. Good evening, I am Vanessa Evangeline Jones." Mrs. Jones shook my Mom's hand awkwardly long and then Mrs. Jones rubbed her hands together with hand sanitizer. I could tell she was a little uppity. "But call me Mrs. Jones. Only my *friends*," she added coldly, "call me Vanessa. I am so glad your daughter Zoey invited my daughter Maddie to your distinctive residence. It has... personality. But now that we are here we can see that you are quite busy, so I suppose I will just cancel my tickets to the symphony and stay home."

"Mom, please, please. I really want to spend the night, *please*," Maddie begged.

"It's no problem," my mother said to the lady. "Really. Enjoy your *symphony*."

"Oh, fabulous." Mrs. Jones gave in. "Good day." She left

without hugging her daughter goodbye with her head held up high in the air.

After Mom went into her room, I said, "So what do you want to do, Maddie? I'd like to draw, because my punishment that included no drawing is over. But I did get to draw at art class every day, except weekends. On weekends I'd just look at my how-to-draw book, and how it was mocking me."

"OK, let's draw."

We went into my room and drew six pictures between the two of us. We soon got hungry, so it was time for us to make my famous chocolate pancakes. Maddie decided to have us both work on the batter and she'd put them on the griddle and flip them.

Before I started working on the chocolate pancake batter, I put on my pink apron Carly had given me.

When I was putting the flour in with my hands Maddie said, "I wonder how flour tastes."

"Oh, you don't want to taste it," I warned. "It tastes awful; I've had it before; It's dry and yuck! But it tastes good when you put all the other ingredients with it. I think the chocolate milk makes it taste less dry and more yum! Chocolate milk's my secret ingredient; it makes the pancakes chocolate pancakes. By the way, don't tell anyone my secret ingredient. The sugar also makes the pancakes taste good; I put in extra.

The more, the better the pancakes."

"Hmm, well it may not taste good by itself, but it's fun to play with by itself!" Maddie tossed some flour on my face. She then started laughing so I threw flour all over her face too. We went back and forth until we were covered from head to toe in flour.

Mom walked in and made us clean up before we could finish cooking. We offered my parents (and even Zach) a plateful of chocolate pancakes, but they all politely declined and ate peanut butter and jelly sandwiches instead. *Their loss. More for us*, we thought. We had five pancakes each.

When Maddie bit into her first pancake, her brown eyes lit up like stars. "These are fantastic! I bet we could sell them. I have experience with my lemonade stand. I can take care of the pricing, advertising, and everything."

"That sounds like a great idea. We can do it in my front yard, do a jingle, and even ask Carly to help. Let's name the business 'Zoey and Maddie's Famous Pancake Stand'! I got the idea from 'Frank's Famous Falafels'. I absolutely adore their jingle."

Maddie and I started singing the Frank's Famous Falafel jingle. "Get a falafel, skip that waffle. Get a Frank's *Famous* Falafel."

"I also love Frank's Famous Falafels. Mom says their

food's gross, because it's fast food, but I still love it," Maddie said.

I knew right at that moment that Maddie and I would be best friends. She wanted to start a business with my amazing chocolate pancakes, she loved to draw zebras, and she totally demolished our kitchen. We were two peas in a pod.

6

Businesses

I was at the doctor's office about to get my cast removed and would no longer have crutches. Dr. Graham told me I would still have to have a brace and take it easy, though. I stared at my brace. It looked worse than my cast. I said, "It looks like a ski boot! Have you ever heard the story of how I broke my leg?"

"Only five times," Dr. Graham mumbled.

After I finished telling Dr. Graham how I broke my leg again, Maddie came over to work on our pancake business. We already came up with a jingle for Zoey and Maddie's Famous Pancake Stand. The jingle was, "Skip that protein shake, and get a pancake at Zoey and Maddie's Famous Pancake Stand." Maddie made a reasonable price for a plate of the best pancakes ever, five dollars for a plate of three pancakes. I created the logo and drew it on the other side of an old banner that was lying around the house from Zach's baby shower. The logo was a pancake being flipped on a spatula. We would hang the banner on two cardboard boxes that we would use as a table. That night Carly would come over, and help Maddie and I cook our pancakes for the next day. We would precook the pancakes, so we wouldn't have to wake up at five o' clock.

When Maddie entered Mom said, "Hi Maddie, did your Mom drop you off?"

"No ma'am, I walked here myself. My mom is busy watching my Dad play in a golf tournament at the country club," Maddie politely answered.

"Yes," Mom whispered. "Carly had to cancel. She has to study for an exam."

"OK, we'll still make great pancakes without her. Did you know Carly's great at cooking? She makes the best macaroni and cheese, she even has a secret ingredient; it's- Oh, I forgot, it's a secret. My secret ingredient is..." I paused to see if anyone was listening before whispering, "chocolate milk. Shh. Don't tell anyone."

"Don't worry, I won't honey. Now you two have a fun time. Oh, and don't set the kitchen on fire please."

Maddie and I said, "Yes Ma'am."

We skipped into the kitchen where we prepared the ingredients, made the batter, and put the pancakes on the griddle. When I flipped one of the pancakes over, it flew across the kitchen directly into Zane's mouth (who was eager to catch it and eat it).

We only made thirty pancakes, so I suggested making more, because I was sure a lot of people would want them.

We were about to make the second batch when Maddie suggested, "Hey, maybe we should add something special to this batch. My mom always puts her special fresh pecans from our pecan tree in her special cookie recipe. Maybe we could put some pecans in the pancakes. Then people don't only have the option of delicious original chocolate pancakes, but they also have the option of delicious special pecan chocolate pancakes."

"Great idea Maddie!" I yelled. "This will make our pancakes even more special. I've never had pecans, but once I had a banana muffin with walnuts. The walnuts were OK; they probably weren't fresh. My friend, well not really my friend, Chloe only eats fresh veggies and fruits. I'm not a big fan of veggies, but I do like some types of fruit. Like strawberries, bananas, and mangos. I had my first mango from a farmers' market. I like going to the farmers' market and the flea market. I once found this amazing dining room chair at the flea market; it was zebra print! I wanted to buy it, but even though it was cheap, I still couldn't afford it, and my parents refused to pay the rest for it. My parents believe that they give us a fair allowance, and we should use that money on things we want, instead of them buying whatever we want all the time. I think that's fair, but sometimes I wish they'd pitch in, just a little every now and then. Oh well, maybe they'll get me a chair just like it for my birthday. Last year they really came through and got me the exact art kit that I had been begging for all year. Every time I asked for it they would say, 'It's too expensive'."

Maddie said, "Let's go over to my house to get the pecans."

"OK, I'm sure my mom won't mind us walking over to your house; it's not that far away, and 'Glen Cove' has the lowest amount of robberies in all the neighborhoods in Houston, so it's safe. My mom read that in an article in 'The Houston Weekly'. Did you know 'The Houston Weekly' always has a Sudoku on the back? Well, you probably didn't know that, because you're new here. Why did you move anyway? I bet New York was nice."

"My dad's job was transferred."

"You live on 'Stoneridge Drive', right?" Maddie nodded her head. "OK, I like that street. It has some of the nicest houses in 'Glen Cove'. I like how they're all made of stone. Stone's pretty. I had a teacher named Ms. Stone in second grade, she was nice, young, and pretty."

I was excited, not only because we were going to pick fresh pecans to put in our delicious one-of-a-kind pancakes that would make them stand out even more, but also because I'd get to see Maddie's house. I liked seeing other people's houses. We linked arms and skipped outside together in perfect unison, looking both ways before crossing the street like both our moms always directed us to do. While we walked we sang the jingle to "Frank's Famous Falafels". It was our favorite jingle; it was even better than our "Zoey and Maddie's Famous Pancake Stand" jingle.

We finally reached Maddie's three-story home made of stone, with a black door, a black roof, and a beautiful garden full of red roses lined in perfect little rows. A table was on the front porch with a vase of roses, and ferns were hanging from the portico. The home also had clear windows with black shutters, and a three-car-garage connected to the house with a honeysuckle overhang. The house was beautiful and well managed. The bushes were all trimmed neatly, the grass was mowed, there wasn't a single dead or wilting plant, and the yard had no toys in it (unlike my house).

As I stared at the house, Maddie said, "Let's go to the backyard."

"Sounds good." I hardly paid any attention to Maddie.

Maddie led me to the gate, and inside was a lovely garden. It had a white flower arch connected to a white fence. Maddie took me past the arch and fence, where there were many exquisite flowers, trees, and more. There was even a little creek with a small waterfall. In the middle of the garden stood a tall tree with small green things attached to it, and brown nuts under it. The tree was dark brown, and had branches that stretched out with its green leaves.

Maddie said, "The pecan tree is in the middle of the garden. I love the pecan tree. It came with the house. So did the garden."

"That thing is a pecan tree?!" I shouted. "But it has green stuff attached to it! How can that be a pecan tree?"

Maddie laughed then said, "That green stuff's just the shell I think. My mom told me pecans come in shells, so I guess the green stuff is the shells."

We ran over to the pecan tree, and the pecans under the tree already had their green shells removed.

"Let's get the pecans with the shells already off. They're on the ground," I said. Maddie and I started to pick the pecans off the ground and put them in the basket we brought. "These pecans are pretty big; maybe we should crush them up a little and maybe add some chocolate chips. I know how to crush the pecans up, my mom has a meat hammer at home; we can use that."

"Good idea," Maddie commented and then stopped putting pecans in the basket. "I think we have enough."

"Yeah. I'll carry the basket home. We use it for

decoration sometimes and put fake apples in it. I used to think they were real, and one day I took a big bite out of one and found out it was fake. It kind of hurt my teeth, but I was fine. It hurt a lot less than when I got my tooth pulled at the dentist. They gave me this thing called laughing gas, and I couldn't stop laughing."

When we got home, I smashed the pecans with my mom's meat hammer while Maddie made the batter and put the chocolate chips and pecans in it.

After we finished cooking all of our pancakes Maddie asked, "Where are you going to put the pancakes tonight?"

"I'm just going to put them right here in the middle of the table, so the dogs can't reach them." I said while putting the four plates of pancakes on the table. "Once Noodle ate half my chocolate bar and threw up. I did give the bar to her though, but I couldn't resist her begging. When she was begging, I was doing my homework. I don't really like homework; it's worse than school, and sometimes even tests, but not multiple-choice tests. I *absolutely* do not like and will *never* like multiple-choice. I write on the back of the page now to explain my answer choices, because there are usually only four answers. How can there only be four possible answers to a question? I think there should be infinite possibilities."

"I have to go. Sorry I can't sleep over. My mom doesn't want me here too long, because of last time when I came home with flour on my clothes.

"Bye. Oh, and I'll get everything set up. I already have the cardboard box table, and the banner is in my room. I love the logo I made, but maybe we can change it to a dog catching a pancake. Like what Zane did earlier, that would be hilarious. But it may be what Mrs. Lewis calls 'irrelevant'. Mrs. Lewis also called my last oral report 'irrelevant'. So I may have gotten a little bit off topic, but I don't think I deserved a C. She said she would have given me a D if it weren't for my drawing that I included in my presentation. We were all supposed to write a report about a president and do a visual aid about the president we chose. I just drew a man with a big powdered wig on his head, but it did turn out pretty good."

"Bye, Zoey," Maddie said, then walked away. "Your stories are interesting."

* * *

The next morning I woke up bright and early at six o'clock, unable to go back to sleep, because the excitement of "Zoey and Maddie's Famous Pancake Stand" was going through my head. I hung the banner on the cardboard boxes, put the syrup, forks, butter pads, napkins, chocolate pancakes and chocolate chip pecan chocolate pancakes on the table. Everything looked great.

Two hours later Maddie showed up. She was wearing an

oversized white apron that didn't have a single stain on it. Maddie had written ZOEY AND MADDIE'S FAMOUS PANCAKE STAND on it with bright red marker.

"Hi Zoey. I borrowed my mom's apron and put a little advertisement on it."

"It looks great," I said. "The pancakes look great. The syrup will make them even better. So will the butter, but some people don't like butter on their pancakes. Zach, Dad, and I do, but Zelena and Mom don't. Zelena, Mom, and I like to paint our nails though, but Zach and Dad don't. I like to get my nails done professionally, because they can do little tiny designs. I once tried to do a zebra on my nails with paint but ended up just doing it on my arm."

"Let's start selling."

We sang our jingle to attract attention, "Get a pancake, skip that protein shake, and get a pancake at 'Zoey and Maddie's Famous Pancake Stand'." After fifteen minutes I almost got tired of our jingle, but finally someone stopped at our stand. It was Mrs. Dickson, my Mom's boss at the hair salon. She had big curly blonde hair, seemed like she was older than my Mom, and always wore a lot of red lipstick.

"Oh, hello children!" Mrs. Dickson said. "How adorable. You're selling pancakes. This must be the business your Mom has been telling me about, Zoey."

"Yes ma'am. You should try them, only five dollars per plate. There are three whole chocolate pancakes or chocolate chip pecan chocolate pancakes on each plate. They're practically a steal. We've been working very hard on this business, and you won't want to say no to two adorable hardworking girls. Would you?"

"Of course not. I'll take one plate of chocolate chip pecan chocolate pancakes, you two cute little girls."

"Here you go," Maddie said, after handing Mrs. Dickson a delicious stack of pancakes with syrup.

"Thank you, I'll try them right now." She took a big bite and exclaimed, "Ouch!" Then she said in a funny voice. "I just chipped my tooth I th'nk." Then pulled part of a pecan out of her mouth and said, "Iz thiz a pecan s..shell?" Then grabbed a napkin and put her chipped tooth on it. "How am I gonna go inta work like thiz. I'm telling your Mom about this, Zoey Thong. Ya gonna have ta tell ya ma she haz ta go inta work, I hav ta go ta tha dentiz." Then she walked away.

"Oh no," Maddie said. "I guess the green stuff wasn't the shell. The brown thing over the soft inside was the shell. I better go tell my Mom about this."

"Yeah, me too. Before Mrs. Dickson does," I said, sad to have to tell my Mom I chipped her boss' tooth.

I slowly walked inside and saw Mom sitting on the

couch.

"Hi, honey," Mom said with a smile on her face. "How's your pancake business going?"

"Well, um..... I, I um, just got my, my f.. first uh, customer. It was, was your boss, um," I said.

"Mrs. Dickson?" Mom said, then I nodded my head. "Oh, did you tell her I said hello? She's such a sweet lady."

"Um, uh. Well.........um, uhhh." I hesitated.

"Zoey, this is the first time you've ever been speechless. What's going on Zoey Grace Song?"

"Um, well, you, you have to go into, into work um, today. Mrs. Um, Dickson told me she has um, to go to, the, the d... dentist."

"Well that's weird. Why didn't she tell me she had a dentist appointment earlier, and more importantly, why are you speechless?"

"OK, here's what happened. I sold Mrs. Dickson a plate of pancakes, and when she took a bite of one, she..... she, sort of, chipped, chipped her... her tooth."

"ZOEY GRACE SONG! What did you put in those pancakes?!"

"It could be because I may have left them out all night

on the table or accidently didn't get the shell off of the pecans."

"Pecans! With shells! Leaving them out all night! You should know better. No phone, no T.V, no cooking, and you're going to go to bed at seven o' clock for a week with no dinner."

"Yes ma'am," I said.

"Oh, and no more of this pancake business! You're also giving Mrs. Dickson a refund and apologizing to her. You shouldn't have sold her pancakes that chipped her tooth for five dollars."

"Yes ma'am." I felt really bad for chipping poor Mrs. Dickson's tooth. She had always liked me and was nice. She even laughed about it later when I apologized for chipping her tooth. She told me not to worry and that she had her tooth fixed without costing her a penny, thanks to her dental plan. It is sort of a funny memory, looking back at it, but Mom will never see it that way

Monday after school I was looking at my pancake logo banner in my room, thinking about my failed business. Maddie wanted to start a new business, but I didn't think it would turn out well with our economy in the tank. It seemed like everything I did got me in trouble, and I was tired of it. If Maddie wanted to start a new business, she could do it by herself. I didn't want to ruin her business with the trouble I always seemed to drag around.

In the middle of my deep thought Zelena entered our room. I kind of wanted to be alone but could have used some comforting.

Zelena softly said, "Hi Zoey, are you OK?"

"Actually, not really," I said in a depressed tone. "I feel like everything I do is wrong. I wish I could be good and quiet like you."

"Really? Zoey, I've always admired your outgoing personality and how you're confident in yourself. You may think I'm just your shy, quiet, perfect sister, but I'm insecure, and I feel like I'm always in your shadow."

This stunned me. I never knew that Zelena (my perfect twin who never does anything wrong) admired *me*, her sister (who always gets in trouble and never does anything right).

"I never knew you felt this way. I've sort of admired you also. Remember that time I asked to switch places with you?" Zelena nodded her head. "Well, I did it because I wanted to be good like you. Not only do you never do anything wrong, but everyone likes you. "

Zelena and I hugged over our new bond. She looked at my artwork that hung on my side of the room. Her eyes lit up and she said, "Wait, about that business thing... I have an idea."

Immediately after Zelena told me her brilliant idea, I invited Maddie over so that we all could work on it.

When Maddie came over she said, "Hi Zoey, oh, and hi Zelena. So you have an idea for a business?"

"Actually, it's Zelena's idea. It's a great idea, and I'm pretty sure you'll love it. I did, and I don't think we'll get in trouble with this idea. I'm sorry I didn't want to start another business; I was just afraid I'd mess it up. Now how about you tell Maddie your idea, Zelena."

Zelena said, "Well, um, OK. Well, where do I start? Um, earlier this afternoon I was looking at a few of Zoey's artwork pieces. When I looked at them I thought they were amazing, and I came up with the idea of 'Zoey and Maddie's Art Stand'."

Maddie said, "Really? That's a great idea! I mean, we both love to draw, and I already have a jingle. 'Get some art, be smart, and use the plan of getting some art that comes from the heart, at Zoey and Maddie's Art Stand'. Isn't it a great idea?"

"Needs work, but yah, it is," I said. "Except for the name. It should be called 'Zelena, Zoey, and Maddie's Art Stand'. Your name should be included. We never would have come up with an art stand without you. You may not like to draw, but you can help with organizing it and everything. Making sure we don't sell wet paintings or anything. We could also do specialty orders where people ask us to draw something specific, and we deliver it to them. You can be in charge of delivery; Maddie can also help you with organizing it all; Maddie and I can work on the drawings."

Zelena said, "Really? I'd love to help."

I said, "Then it's settled; our new business will be called, 'Zelena, Zoey, and Maddie's Art Stand'. Let's get started. Zelena, you can work on the prices while Maddie and I work on some paintings; we already have some paintings that we can sell; we have six altogether; I drew four and Maddie drew the rest. I drew more of them, but Maddie's paintings looked at lot better. I drew a golden doodle that looks like Noodle, a zebra, sunflowers, and a bluebird. Maddie drew a beautiful monarch butterfly and waterfall that went into a clear blue lake. I've been wanting to canoe with Sarah in her parent's canoe at the lake, but she's too 'sophisticated' for that now. She told me that when I asked her last week. She and Chloe are going to go to the nail salon today. I would have liked to go. I want to paint my nails pink with tiny flowers on them. I might have gone if they had invited me, or if Chloe wasn't going to be there, or if I hadn't spent all my weekly allowance on candy."

Zelena and I had never been close until our business took flight. Over the next week, she priced each painting at two dollars and took a lot of care setting up our art stand. She put a folding table out in the front yard displaying my paintings and

Maddie's paintings. Zelena also decided to have us make paper frames for the paintings. Once our business was ready, we started selling our pictures on a Saturday. Our first customer was Mrs. Dickson! She was eager to buy a painting of a zebra that I had drawn. She said every time she would look at it, she would think of me.

"Zelena, Zoey, and Maddie's Art Stand" became famous around the neighborhood. We made fifty dollars by the end of the first week. All three of us split the money evenly. I finally realized I could do something without getting into trouble, and Zelena was a lot more fun than I used to think. For a moment, I thought my life was really turning around.

7

Track and Field

ZELENA, Maddie, Sarah, Chloe, and I were all sitting at lunch together. I brought up the topic of me getting my brace off the next day. "Hey, did you know I'm getting my brace off tomorrow? I'm so excited! I want to join some sort of sport. I'm just not sure which sport. I would like to try gymnastics, but I'd like to be on a team with people I know, and if I start now I'll end up with a group of four year olds. So I was thinking about a school team, like cheerleading, but they start at the beginning of the year."

"The track and field team is holding tryouts after school Tuesday," Sarah suggested. "I'm trying out. Maybe you'd like it."

"Sounds fun. I'm pretty good at running, and we can practice at the school's track tomorrow after my doctor's appointment. Maybe I'll tell Dr. Graham the story of how I broke my leg again. He loves the story, at least I think he does; well maybe he doesn't. He never smiles during the story; he always smiles after the story when I'm done telling it and I have to leave."

Zelena said, "I also enjoy running, I'll tryout."

Sarah asked, "What about you, Maddie and Chloe?"

"I'd love to, but I have gymnastics." Maddie said.

"And I hate to sweat." Chloe said then flipped her hair.

I was disappointed that Maddie wouldn't be able to do track and field, but I was glad Sarah and Zelena would try for it. I just didn't want one of them to not make it. I had never really seen Zelena run. I was sure I'd make it though; my leg would be aching to move after being in a cast, then a brace. That would probably make me go faster, I thought.

After school, Zelena and I stretched in the living room to prepare for our practice with Sarah at the school's track. We started out trying to touch our toes, and I was close to my toes.

I said, "This is easy." Then I started to bend my legs a little, and it started to hurt. "Ouch!"

Zelena lifted me back up and asked, "Are you alright?"

"Yah," I answered, massaged my leg. "I just bent it and was doing too much. Don't worry, I'll be fine by tomorrow when I get my brace off. I better just relax and take it easy till then. I'm a little tired also, you can just keep stretching, and I'll just lie down for a while."

"Alright," Zelena said while trying to reach her toes.

I went to my room to lie down on my bed, hoping my leg would heal in time for tryouts. I'd just fit in some intense training between tomorrow and Tuesday, I decided. I would run the school's track with sheer intensity for three hours every day until tryouts.

The next morning, I woke up eager for my doctor's appointment. Zelena came with me for support. After I finished telling Dr. Graham again the story of how I broke my leg, he told me several things to be careful of. While he was telling me about this, I imagined myself getting first place in a track and field competition. I accepted the trophy humbly before delivering a deep and moving speech.

"Thank you, thank you," I said in my speech. "I am honored to accept this award. I will put this trophy on my award shelf to mark my many other prestigious accomplishments. One of my awards is a ribbon for participating in a soccer competition. I always got that award in soccer competitions. My friend, Hannah, always got MVP, most valuable player. Come to think about it, everyone got an award, even Nose Picking Tommy."

After my doctor's appointment I got ready for my practice. I was tying my shiny, unique zebra print running shoes when Mom entered.

"Hi, Zoey," Mom said before sitting down on my bed. "Take it easy please. Remember what the doctor said. Try not to do too much at once. Zelena told me about what happened yesterday while you were stretching."

"Don't worry, Mom. I won't do too much," I assured her, with the plan of my training still in my mind. "I've learned my lesson. Speaking of lessons, Ms. Shannon, my Math teacher was teaching us about some boring lesson and then she got a call from her daughter who needed her to pick her up, because she got suspended. Ms. Shannon said, 'You got suspended!' While on the phone with her daughter. Our teacher ran out and then a substitute teacher came after five minutes of chaos. She played a bunch of videos about how to do math problems."

"OK, just be careful," Mom advised with a worried expression on her face.

Zelena walked in already geared up and said, "Hi Zoey, are you ready? Sarah is waiting for us at the track."

"I'm ready. Bye Mom. Oh, and can we have lasagna for dinner? I love lasagna almost as much as Carly's mac and cheese or my pancakes. Too bad my pancake business didn't work out. I loved the jingle, and the merchandise was genius. It was also fun to cook the pancakes, but it's also fun to make my merchandise for my art stand."

"I'll cook lasagna, I guess. Bye and good luck."

"Bye Mom!" Zelena said.

She and I linked arms and skipped into my parent's old van. Zach and Dad were already in the van. Everything was going well until I realized Zach was in the driver's seat! He was about to drive when I shouted, "STOP! Zach, are you about to drive? You don't even have your license. How could you allow this to happen, Dad? Don't you love us and care about our safety?!"

Dad said, "Don't worry, Zach just got his learner's permit. He's only going to drive out of the neighborhood, then I'll drive."

Zelena politely said, "I am sure he will do fine."

"Oh, and I just want you guys to know that, this is the first time I've ever driven, so I wanna be careful," Zach warned us before slowly driving out of the driveway.

"Zach!" Zelena exclaimed. "You're going too slow. You can't go that slow or you might get a ticket."

"She's right. Zach, let me drive," Dad said.

"Fine," Zach said then switched seats with Dad.

While Dad cautiously drove and pointed out his "technique" to Zach, I looked at my legs. My leg that I had broken looked weaker and smaller than the other leg. Maybe if I exercised my weaker leg more than my other leg, it would be as strong as my other leg.

We finally reached the school where Sarah was already zooming around the track. Zelena and I got out of the car and watched Sarah.

"Wow, she's good," Zelena commented.

"Yah, but we're better," I said. "Wanna start running? My leg can't wait to start running again. My leg I broke looks weaker, but I'll be fine. Let's start moving; let's race to see who can get to the track first."

"You're on."

We both darted to the track trying to beat each other. Zelena was a lot faster than I expected. She ran ahead of me, so I had to speed up. I gave it my all and ran ahead of Zelena. My leg started to ache, but I pushed through and made it to the track as the victor.

Sarah ran towards us and started to slow down. "Hi guys, how's your leg feeling Zoey?"

"Good. A little sore, but I just beat Zelena at a race. She's pretty good; you should try to race her. Hey, here's an idea, what if we all race each other? It'll be great practice, and a lot of fun. There needs to be a prize though. Hmm...."

Sarah suggested, "How about losers have to do winner's science homework for a week. We all hate science."

Zelena said, "I actually quite like science."

I added, "Plus my teacher's going to think something's up if you both do my homework. What about... losers have to give their desserts to the winner at lunch on Monday. Our lunch lady's making her signature banana pudding; Make sure to get me one with extra bananas please, when I win. If you beg and make a sad look on your face, she'll give you the one with the most bananas. Hey, did you know that monkeys love bananas, but chimpanzees like grapes more? They still eat bananas though. Have you seen that movie *Crazy Chimpanzees*? Hannah's aunt's doctor's sister's aerobics class teacher's dentist's son's best friend's basketball teammate's great grandfather's caregiver's favorite hair stylist's baby loves that movie."

Sarah said, "I haven't seen that movie, but that's a great idea for a prize."

"I think so too," Zelena said while nodding her head.

"Well, let's start," Sarah said. "Ready... set... GO!"

I started running on my leg that was still aching. I began

with a great amount of speed, running ahead of everyone. It felt glorious until I was out of breath and my leg started to hurt so much I had to sit down in the middle of the track. Zelena and Sarah quickly stopped and ran over to me.

"Are you alright?" Zelena asked.

"You might just be dehydrated. I have some water in my bag, I'll go get it." Sarah started running towards her bag.

"No, I'm fine," I said. Sarah stopped running. "It's my leg, I just need a little break. You can both continue with the race. But since I'm no longer participating, do I need to still give the winner my dessert? If so, that's fine, I always find a way to sneak a second one, then sometimes a third."

"We don't need to finish the race, it wouldn't be fair to you. Right, Zelena?"

"Right. I could actually use a break, I'm not used to running this much." Zelena sat down next to me.

"Me either." Sarah sat down.

After our short break, we went back to running. My leg kept hurting, and the more it hurt, the more I ignored it. After ten minutes of running nonstop I tripped and fell down, and felt a sharp pain in my leg. I cried and Zelena and Sarah ran right over.

Zelena shouted, "Zoey! Are you OK?!"

"No," I struggled to say through the pain.

"I'll call Dad right away." She pulled her phone out of her pocket and called Dad. I waited for her to finish the short phone call that seemed like it lasted for hours.

"So, is he coming?" Sarah asked, which added to the anxiety.

"Well, um actually, kind of, um, no, but he told me we should get help immediately, and go to the hospital."

"What?!" I yelled.

"Our old car got into a little wreck while Zach was driving. But no one's hurt, and the car's at the repair shop," Zelena said.

"Then who's going to come?!" I yelled in pain.

"I'll call my Dad," Sarah said.

Sarah's Dad finally came and drove us to the hospital. When we got there Zach and Dad were there too! Zach had a ginormous red bump on his forehead! It kind of looked like an extreme zit. He was screaming in pain, with tears in his eyes. He was in such pain that he didn't even notice us, but Dad did and shouted, "ZOEY!" Then he apologized for not picking me up a million times.

I said in pain, "It's fine, just get me to a doctor!"

I was taken to a doctor, and he put my brace back on. And that giant bump on Zach's head was from knocking his head in the car wreck. Thank goodness no one was seriously hurt, but the car was taken to the repair shop. After I had my brace put back on, I realized I couldn't tryout for track and field with a brace!

It wasn't fair. I wanted to tryout for track and field at my school on Tuesday. My two best friends were doing it. I had been dreaming about track and field since just the day before! Why could Sarah and Zelena try out, but I couldn't? I was even better than both of them, but I couldn't even try out until 7th grade. *They'll both be a lot better than me and are going to make new friends*, I thought.

I didn't say a word during the entire ride home. I was so mad that I didn't get to do track and field, but Zelena who was not even as good as me could. I deserved to tryout as much as Sarah and Zelena, probably even more.

When we got home Mom was waiting for us. "Hi sweetie, are you OK?"

"I'm fine," I quietly said, but I really was not fine. "I'm going to go call Maddie. She'll want to know what happened."

"That's fine, dinner's almost ready. One of your favorites, remember? Lasagna!" Mom said.

I walked into my room depressed. I couldn't wait to just

pour out all my feelings on Maddie; she always understood me. I called and waited for her to answer, but she didn't answer. I tried to call her again, but she still didn't answer. I plopped down on my bed and thought about my lost dreams of track and field.

"Zoey! Zach! Dinner's ready!" Mom called from the kitchen.

I walked into the kitchen while Zach ran. Zelena was already seated at the table with her napkin in her lap.

Zelena said, "May I please have a glass of water? I dislike having to trouble any of you, but my throat is quite dehydrated from the stroll today."

I rolled my eyes, then Dad handed Zelena a glass of water.

"May I say grace?" Zelena asked.

"Of course sweetheart," Mom said.

Zelena said a perfectly elegant prayer.

"Now time to chow down," Zach announced, then took a giant bite of lasagna.

Zelena said. "You are showing very poor table manners Zach."

Dad agreed, "Zelena's right. Eat smaller bites."

Zach took a regular bite and said, "Better?"

"Thank you," Zelena said before taking a dainty bite of her corn.

I rolled my eyes again, irritated at Zelena being so perfect. Not only was she perfect, she got everything she wanted. Not having Zach gorge his food in front of her, track team tryouts, a glass of water, because of her "dehydration", and she got to say prayers. I also had a very good prayer in mind.

I played around with my food, because for the first time in my life I was not hungry.

When dinner was over and Mom was about to take my plate, she said, "Honey, you didn't eat anything. You also were very quiet during dinner, are you feeling alright?"

"Yes, I'm just not hungry."

"I'll eat her food." Zach volunteered then took my plate.

Mom said, "Zoey, at least eat the corn."

"Yes ma'am." I ate my corn.

* * *

The next day at church I entered my Sunday school class and sat down next to Maddie, who had a shocked expression on her face. Zelena never went to kid's church. She preferred adult church. It was the perfect time to tell Maddie how I felt.

She said, "Zoey! What happened? I thought you got your brace off yesterday."

"Hi Maddie," I said. "I was running the track with Sarah and Zelena, and my leg started to hurt, so we went to the doctor and he said I needed my brace again. It's not fair; I'm a better runner than Zelena, but I don't get to tryout. It's like she gets everything because she's perfect."

"I'm sorry, I hope you feel better."

After church my family and I went home in a nice, new car. It was wonderful to ride in a car without paint on the windows, dirt scattered on the floor, and marker on the ceiling. Too bad it would only last till two o' clock that day. The car place only gave us that car until they fixed our other one.

At home Mom made us lunch. I was starving from not eating anything but corn the night before. My talk with Maddie had cheered me up, and I was back to the old me. I was even thinking about talking to Zelena again; it wasn't her fault I hurt my leg. Right then, Zelena entered the kitchen wearing her running shoes and had her hair back in a ponytail. Was she going running? She couldn't be; it wouldn't be fair.

"Hi Mom." Zelena said. "May I please skip lunch, I want to practice running around the neighborhood. I need to practice for track and field tryouts."

"Alright, that's fine. Just be careful, and come back by at least two o' clock."

"Thank you."

That was it. I had lost my appetite. I forgot that Zelena was still going to try out even though I couldn't.

I asked, "May I be excused?"

Mom said, "Yes, you may. Are you OK? You haven't been eating lately?"

"I've just not been hungry."

I walked over to Zelena and said, "We need to talk."

"Alright."

We walked into our room.

"What do you want to talk about? I'm about to go run."

"I know. How could you do this?"

"Do what?"

"How could you still tryout for track without me? Why do you still get to tryout? Just because you didn't break your leg? It's not fair."

"I'm sorry, but just because you injured yourself and

can't tryout doesn't mean I can't. Zoey, you got to do soccer. You got to do the fun and important stuff at the art cart while I just organized it like a secretary. When you broke your leg, everyone focused on you. Carrying your books, signing your cast, and asking what happened. This is the first time people will focus on me as me, instead of Zoey's twin who switched places with her when Zoey blew blue chemicals all over the science lab."

Suddenly, I felt bad. Zelena had supported me by not letting me give up doing my own businesses, and even came up with a new business and helped me with it.

"I'm sorry. I haven't been the best sister lately. I should support you with track and field instead of wanting you to not do it. You have always supported me, and I have never supported you; I've been selfish. You even went along with my plan to switch places, just because I wanted Mrs. Lewis to like me. For once in my life, I'll support you. I'll come to your tryout and cheer you on."

"Really? Thank you, Zoey."

We hugged. I finally realized that Zelena did deserve to try out. She was a good runner and a hard worker.

There was more good news. They couldn't fix our old car, so my parents just bought the shiny new car they gave us. Everything had turned out great. I didn't need a sport; I already had my art stand. I'd also be busy cheering on Zelena in her track and field competitions if she made the team.

On Tuesday, Zelena was ready for tryouts after practicing hard. She told me at lunch she didn't focus on her lessons for the first time in her life. She said she was anxious, but I reassured her that she would do fine.

After a long day of school, it was finally time for tryouts. I was so happy for Zelena, I even invited Maddie to cheer on her and Sarah. There were thirty people trying out, and only ten people would make it. So only one-third of the people would make the team. The coach gave the thirty people a speech before beginning. I held up my 'Go Zelena' sign that was pink and covered in glitter. Zelena started out a little slow, but she began to speed up and was in the front of the crowd of people running. The coach was naming everyone who made the team, and the last name was Zelena!

After tryouts, Zelena ran over and hugged me.

"We need to celebrate," I said. "Maybe with ice cream sundaes! I'd like mine with a scoop of strawberry ice cream, a scoop of chocolate ice cream, and a scoop of vanilla ice cream, with bananas, whipped cream, sprinkles, hot fudge, big chunks of cookie dough, strawberries, and caramel sauce on top. No cherry, though. I don't want to stuff myself."

"Or maybe we could just have vanilla ice cream with hot fudge. You can come Maddie, and let's invite Sarah. She also made the team," Zelena said.

Sarah, Zelena, Maddie and I had an ice cream sundae party to celebrate. I was so happy for both of them. They deserved it. And even though I didn't get to tryout, there's always next year.

8

Work

I was in Mrs. Lewis' boring ELA class. It had just begun. She was rambling on about some news as I doodled on my notebook paper, which was meant for taking notes. By the time class was over, I had already doodled on four pieces of paper. I do participate in class when Mrs. Lewis asks us questions, but she never calls on me. *I wonder why.* I walked out of class and to my locker. Zelena was nearby.

She noticed me and said, "Hi Zoey. Pretty exciting news that Mrs. Lewis said at the beginning of class."

"Well, what was the news? I was busy drawing. I drew the perfect circle; I tried to draw more circles like it, but I couldn't. I guess no two circles are alike, like snowflakes. I wish it could snow in Texas; I like the snow when we visit Colorado, but it doesn't snow all the time in Colorado, or even Alaska. Well maybe in some parts it snows all the time."

"The news was, that tomorrow is bring your kid to work day at our school."

"It is? I'd love to go to work with Mom. The only thing is that just looking at Mrs. Dickson reminds me of my failed pancake business. I can deal with her for one day, I guess. I like the hair salon a lot better than school. At least I can learn something important at the hair salon, like you should always get a trim every once in a while or you'll get split ends. Well, bye, my art class is about to start."

"Bye."

At dinner that night, I wanted to ask Mom if I could go to work with her.

After Dad said grace, he asked, "So did anything interesting happen at school today?"

I was about to tell everyone about bring your kid to work day, but then Zach said, "I got hit on the head with a dodge ball; had to go to the nurse."

Mom replied, "I'm sorry, honey. Next time can you tell Bertha I said hello?"

"Sure."

"Tomorrow's bring your kid to work day!" I finally got to say. "I was wondering if I could go to the hair salon with you, Mom. Maybe I can learn how to professionally dye hair. I can also recommend hairstyles for the customers. Maybe I'll end up with a part time job there!"

Mom said, "I'm sorry, Zoey, but I don't think you'll learn much there. Maybe you can go to work with your Dad instead. You'll learn a lot more from him."

Dun dun dun dun! This was not good. It would have been good if he had an interesting job, but he did not have an interesting job. He was a college professor! I didn't even know what he taught!

"I'd love to go to work with Dad. May I, please?" Zelena pleaded.

Dad answered, "Of course you can."

Great. I figured if Zelena wants to go, whatever Dad teaches is probably not interesting.

Mom said, "What a fun learning experience you'll both have."

Learning was even worse than not interesting. Something told me Dad did not teach something fun and interesting like art. I would probably *not* have a fun time.

Later that night, exactly seventeen minutes past my bedtime, I was texting Maddie when Zelena was asleep and I was still awake. Sometimes I'd text Maddie past my bedtime when Zelena was asleep and couldn't tell on me. I honestly preferred calling, because I have a lot to type when I text, but my parents would hear me if I called. I told Maddie about me going with my Dad to work in the morning, what my Dad did, and a few other topics. Maddie texted me back, telling me about how she was going to work with her Mother, who owned an interior design company. Lucky Maddie, she got to do something creative and fun while I did something dull and lifeless.

The next morning I wanted to wear my zebra print shirt, but Mom insisted on me wearing more "suitable" clothes. I settled on my red long-sleeved shirt that said ZOEY on it. Zelena wore her hair up in a bun, had a black pencil skirt on, and a white long sleeved blouse. She looked like she was going to teach the class. Although with her brains, maybe she was.

We drove to the college, which bustled with hundreds of college students rushing to their classes. We entered a large classroom, which was full of unhappy faces, waiting for class to start.

"Hello everyone," Dad said. "My twin daughters are here for bring your kid to work day, so they will quietly observe the class. Now you two go sit down, please."

"Yes, sir." We sat next to each other in two empty seats on the front row.

I promised to be on my best behavior and was sticking to the agreement *so far.*

Dad began class by saying. "Good morning, zoology class-"

I interrupted him. "Zoology! So that's what you teach, Daddy? I wasn't sure what you taught. I was hoping art, but you don't seem that artistic, unless zoology is a type of art or something. I've never heard of it though, but I never heard of abstract art until yesterday in Ms. Crystal's class."

"Excuse my daughter. She's just curious about the exciting world of zoology, which is about *animals-*"

"Oh, animals," I interrupted again. "I love animals; we have two dogs at home. We also have Zach, but according to Zelena he's not an animal, he just acts like one. My favorite animals are zebras. I wanted to wear my zebra print shirt, but my Mom wouldn't let me. I settled on this shirt that says my name on it. Zelena has a shirt just like it, except it has her name on it. She's not wearing it right now though. She's wearing a more professional looking outfit."

Dad said, "Excuse me, I have to have a private talk with my daughter." He took me out to the hall and did not look happy. "You said you'd be on your best behavior. No more interruptions. It's very distracting to the entire room full of people who actually care about zoology," Dad warned.

"Yes sir."

I took my seat again and quietly listened to my Dad as he taught us about classifying animals. This lasted for around five minutes. All I had learned was to never take zoology in college. I was already bored to tears, so I looked over at a young lady sitting next to me with blond straight hair, gray eyes, and tanned skin. She was writing in her notebook. I thought she was taking notes before she ripped out the piece of paper, folded it, and handed it to a cute guy next to her. He smiled. She shyly smiled back. I wondered if the girl liked him. She must have been passing a note. Great idea! Such a thing doesn't distract the entire class, and I can still communicate with people.

I wrote a note to the girl next to me who was still passing notes to the boy next to her:

Hello. I'm Zoey. What's your name? I'm the professor's daughter. I'm here because of bring your kid to work day. I wanted to go to the hair salon with my Mom, but my parents said I'd learn more if I came here. I'm sorry you have to come here everyday. It's really boring here. I can see why you're passing notes. I saw you pass that note to the cute guy next to you. Do you like him? Oh, and thanks for the idea of passing notes.

The girl blushed while reading the note, then put on a straight face. She leaned over to me and whispered, "Stop. You're going to get us both in trouble."

I said, "Don't worry, I'm used to that. So, do you like

that guy next to you?"

"Shhh," she said quietly and stopped passing notes to the guy and focused on my Dad teaching.

If she was too shy to tell me if they liked each other, I thought to ask the boy myself.

I quickly wrote a note to the boy:

Hi, I'm Zoey. I sit next to the girl who was passing notes to you. About that girl, does she like you? She won't tell me, but she seems like she likes you. If you don't already like each other, I think you two would be a perfect couple. She's pretty, you're handsome, and you both share an interest in zoology.

I crumbled the piece of paper up in a ball and passed it to the girl next to me and said, "To the boy next to you."

"Zoey!" My Dad yelled.

Oops! Maybe I should of said that quieter.

"Are you passing a note, Zoey? Let me see it." Dad snatched the crumpled note from my hand. He un-crumpled it and read what it said, "Out in the hall, now!"

"Yes sir," I said then walked into the hall.

There was a clock out in the hall that said 9:45. I assumed my Dad would come out and talk to me again, but I waited for five minutes and he still wasn't there. I waited five more minutes, and he still wasn't there. I guessed he was not coming, so I had to entertain myself. I had a nice chat with myself about if the girl and the boy liked each other. I love talking to myself, but sometimes, I talk a little too much.

I looked at the clock, and it was finally 10:30, time for my Dad's class to end. A large group of students charged out of the classroom. Dad walked out after the crowd left.

He said, "Zoey. I want to talk to you about what happened earlier. I was honestly disappointed you didn't find my class interesting. I was hoping you'd enjoy my class. I know you love animals, and I thought you'd like learning more about them. I guess it wasn't and that's fine."

I said, "Wait, Dad. I'm sorry I was passing notes. Maybe I didn't give your class a chance. At the next class, you'll have my full attention."

"Really? Maybe you'll like it. I wanted you to admire my job just as much as you admire your Mom's job."

"I do like your job. I just don't like school. I'll give it another chance, and even if it is a little boring, I won't distract your class."

"Thank you. Now let's go. My next class is about to start."

"OK. By the way, could you possibly include zebras in your lesson, or dogs? Oh, and do you know if zebras are white with black stripes, or black with white stripes?"

As we started to walk back in the classroom Dad said, "Zebras are black with white stripes." I was happy to finally get an answer. I had wondered about it for years.

Dad was actually smart and his lesson was pretty interesting. You'll never guess what he did. He dissected a frog to show its body parts! Of course, he didn't dye its skin blue, but it was fun to see it done the "right" way. I listened to the entire lecture in all of his other classes.

* * *

At lunchtime, I got my lunch and was about to sit with my Dad and Zelena when the girl who was passing notes to the boy called me over. I sat down on the empty seat, wondering why she wanted to talk to me. *Was she mad?*

"Hi, Zoey. Thanks for writing that note to the boy next to me. Your Dad, Professor Song, gave him the note after class. I've actually had a crush on him for a while, and after reading that note, he told me he also likes me."

I said, "Really? I'm glad everything worked out. Things worked out pretty good for me also. My Dad's class is actually interesting. I don't want to be a zoologist or whatever when I grow up, but I finally found something I like to learn about."

"That's great."

Then the boy appeared.

"Hey, Savannah," the boy said. "Hey, it's the girl who wrote me the note."

"Hey, Devan. Yep, this is Zoey. Um, Zoey, would you mind if Devan sat there?" Savannah said and then winked at me.

"No, I'll just go sit with my sister and Dad. Nice meeting you both. I'm glad I came here for bring your kid to work day. It's been interesting, even more interesting than hair salon gossip. Well, bye. I hope I'll see you soon," I said then walked away.

I was happy one of my mischievous adventures had made two young college students admit their true feelings about each other.

At dinner I shared everything that happened, except Devan and Savannah's true love. That would be my little secret.

Dad said to Zach, "All this talk about careers is starting to worry me, that you aren't ever going to decide what you want to do. You're almost seventeen, and college isn't far away."

Zach said, "Don't worry, I'll just be a 'Science Geeks' video game player. But if that doesn't work out, I have something solid to fall back on: football.”

I said, “I have a few jobs in mind. You can be a slug farmer, or a toilet paper tester, maybe a clown. Chloe says her uncle's a clown, because he always is tripping and falling. I wonder if Chloe's uncle can throw a pie in my face; I've always wanted to lick pie off my face. Although last week I smashed the cafeteria's chocolate pudding all over my face, and everyone at my lunch table said it was disgusting. Chloe gagged, then said, ‘You have no dignity, Zoey Grace Song.’ I'm fine with Chloe thinking I'm disgusting; she disgusts me.”

Mom exclaimed, “Zoey! First of all, Chloe is a perfectly fine, lovely, and sweet girl. Second of all, stop smashing food on your face. Third of all, how could you suggest those jobs to your brother?”

“Do you not like those jobs? Here's some more then; maybe you'll like these. Cheese sculptor, security guard at the world's largest jar of peanut butter, men's chest-hair-waxer, or a foot fungus doctor. See Zach, there's a ton of jobs you'd be great at.”

“Zoey!” Dad said, “Your Mom told you not to say stuff like that, and don't bring up foot fungus at the dinner table.”

“Yes, sir.” I didn't bring up any more jobs for Zach, but I still had one job left in my mind: a deodorant sampler.

9

Star Scouts

I got my brace off again, finally, but instead of being excited this time, I realized I had no sport or activity to do. Being at Zelena's first track and field competition made me think about that even more. I held up my 'Go Zelena' sign, while she sped to the front and finished in first place. Sarah humbly accepted third place, celebrating her friend's victory. I told Zelena I was proud of her, and I really was. She had finally found something she loved and was good at. While I, on the other hand, only had my art stand.

Business was booming when I first created it, but people began to care less about it. I would watch cars pass by, as if they had not even seen it. Maddie and Zelena quit the art stand, because Zelena had track and field and "Help Houston Stay Clean", and Maddie had gymnastics.

One afternoon, when all my friends were busy, I looked out my bedroom window at the backyard, where it was sunny and a swing set was waiting for me to play. Most days I would automatically go outside and try to swing to the sky, but that day I didn't feel like I usually felt. I couldn't help but think about the big smile on Zelena's face when she had won the race. I wasn't jealous of her; I just wanted to love something as much as Zelena loved track and field. All my friends were doing something they loved, while I looked outside at an empty swing.

Mom walked in, raised her eyebrow, and said, "Um, Zoey, are you OK? You're quietly sitting on your bed, looking out a window. Did you switch places again? Is Zoey at your track and field practice right now?"

"No," I answered. "I'm Zoey, not Zelena. Zelena and the rest of my friends are busy doing something. I'm kind of bored. I don't do a sport or activity. My art stand business hasn't had a customer the entire week. No matter how long, or how high I wave my hands to people passing by, no one notices me."

"Hmm. This is perfect timing. Your cousin Carly is an honorary Star Scout, so she's going to start volunteering at our local Star Scout troop next week. Perhaps you'd like to be a Star Scout. I also did it and made it to the highest rank. It's for girls, and you get to sell brownies, go camping, and earn badges."

I hopped up off of my bed with joy, and said, "I can't wait to start! Not only will I get to camp, which I haven't done in years, but I'll also get to spend more time with Carly. Is she going to be the head Scout leader? She would be great with all those charts and graphs she does to keep things organized."

"Well, Carly is not the Scout master, but I think my old one, Ms. June, is still the Scout master. She's the sweetest person I've ever met. You'll love her. I'll try to sign you up tonight."

Yippy! I got to do Star Scouts with a nice Scoutmaster and, most importantly, I got to do Star Scouts!

I said, "Thank you so much, Mom! I better start packing for the next camping trip. I better get my toothbrush, tent, clothes, and super fluffy pillow for pillow fights-"

"Wait, keep in mind you may not be able to do Star Scouts. Most people start at the beginning of the year," Mom warned, but I hardly listened, because I was too excited about Star Scouts.

I was already imagining me with my hundreds of badges. I would go to the highest rank like my Mom and Carly did. I would be the best. Scout. *Ever*.

On the bus the next day, Maddie sat beside me as usual.

"Hi Maddie," I said. "Guess what? My mom signed me up for Star Scouts! Well not officially, but I'll be signed up by this afternoon if things work out. I can't wait. I love camping; I'll get to do lots of that at scouts; I already packed my stuff for a camping trip. I'm not sure when we're going camping though. I packed my zebra stuffed animals, Mrs. and Mr. Stripes. I also have a giant teddy bear, a puppy, and giraffe stuffed animal, but I don't want to over pack."

"Sounds fun. Hey, let's practice camping in your backyard."

"Great idea. We can invite Zelena, have fun as friends, make S'mores, and enjoy the beautiful outdoors. What video game do you want to bring? I'm bringing my new one, 'Virtual Outdoors', and 'S'more Maker'."

We planned our big night the rest of the school day. When I got home, Mom had a huge smile on her face. She said, "Zoey, I got you signed up for Star Scouts. You'll start next week. You'll start in the lowest rank, which is bronze. There are four ranks: bronze, silver, gold, platinum, and diamond."

I couldn't wait for diamond; last time I tried to get diamonds I broke my leg.

I would make it to the diamond rank without breaking either leg.

*
＊ ＊

I helped Zelena pack for our camping trip on Saturday. We packed clothes, her toothbrush and toothpaste, her brush, video games, and computer. We decided to pack lightly. Then

Maddie came over with a suitcase.

Mom said, "Hi Maddie. That's a big suitcase for one night. What's in it?"

"Just all of my video games, several of my favorite movies, and the other essentials."

"Girls, what all did you pack? In my Scout days, we would only bring what we absolutely needed. Now, unpack all of those unnecessary things, and I'll take them, and you'll get them back tomorrow."

Mom took all of our "unnecessary" things and gave us a board game. Even though we didn't have our movies or video games, we'd still have fun. We had marshmallows, chocolate, and graham crackers. Everyone has fun with S'mores.

After Mom repacked us, we went outside where my Dad had pitched my tiny pink tent. When we would camp as a family, they would put Zelena and me in that tent, but we had not gone camping since we were six. After Maddie's giant suitcase, Zelena's small suitcase, and my big duffle bag were in the tent, it was a little crowded (even without any of us in it).

"So, what do you guys want to do?" Maddie asked.

I said, "Um, we can uh, I don't know. I'm not used to being without my video games. We can jump rope, I guess. Or um, swing, or play 'ring around the rosy'. What am I talking about? I haven't played that in years; I'm losing my mind without my video games!"

Zelena suggested, "We can make S'mores. Let's start on the fire."

I said, "OK, I'll get the wood, and then I'll rub two sticks together, to create a fire. There are a ton of little twigs from Mr. Carson's tree that land in our yard. His tree grows flowers during spring; they're pink. I found a cute pair of pink sneakers at the thrift store yesterday. I'm saving up to buy them; I want to wear them at school on Monday with my white shorts and pink and white striped shirt I'm planning to wear. Mom told me if I wear those white shorts, I can't stain them or get them dirty."

I got out of the tent and walked on the mud that was damp and mushy from the previous night. I jumped up and down in the mud, getting the mud all the way up to my ankles. Then I gathered a good-sized pile of twigs. I dropped the pile of twigs in front of the tent, then picked two up and started rubbing the two sticks together. Not a single spark lit, so I decided to rub harder. Still nothing. I rubbed harder and harder until the twigs broke in half!

Zelena said, "Um, Zoey dear, I don't think you can start a fire with tiny twigs. I think you need matches."

"I'll just try again with stronger twigs," I said, "I'm sure I can start a simple fire. I *am* planning to be a diamond scout. Mom and Carly were also Star Scouts. In fact, Carly's volunteering to help with Star Scouts. I'm sure she'll be great as long as she's her fun self instead of her responsible self."

I found the biggest twigs I could find and then rubbed them together even harder than before. After accidently breaking ten twigs, I gave up and threw down my sticks. "That's it! We're having cold S'mores! I'm sorry. After we have our cold S'mores, let's throw the Frisbee. I can throw really hard. I love to play with Zane and Noodle. Zane is a better catcher, but Noodle actually brings the Frisbee back. Mr. Carson's dog, Winston, is a great catcher; he brings the Frisbee back; he even entered a Frisbee catching contest at the park. A young golden retriever named Bella won, but Winston got third place. Bella is Ms. Robin's dog; she got her three years ago."

I ate four cold S'mores, while Zelena and Maddie only ate one. After our S'mores, we threw the Frisbee. When it was my turn to throw it, I accidently threw it over the fence.

"Zoey!" Maddie exclaimed. "You threw it. You get it."

I climbed over the wooden fence and got a splinter in my hand. I ignored the splinter, then got the Frisbee and threw the Frisbee over the fence. I started to climb the fence again, but I remembered the gate on the side. I unlocked the gate, opened it, and walked back into our backyard, assuming the gate had closed behind me.

After we continued playing Frisbee, we swung on the swing and complained about missing our electronics. Then it started to get dark, so we set up our sleeping bags. With our sleeping bags and bags, the tent had no extra room. We lay inside our sleeping bags, trying to go to sleep. We couldn't; it was crowded, freezing cold, and the ground was hard.

Zelena sat up and said, "How are we going to sleep like this?"

"I don't know. I'm so cold," Maddie said while shivering.

While they were saying this, a plan was brewing in my mind. I said, "Hmm. Let's sneak inside and sleep there. We'll wake up early, come out here, and say we slept here all night. Everyone's asleep, so they won't notice. Zach's snoring is probably louder than us coming back in."

"OK, good idea," Maddie complimented.

Zelena said, "I'm not sure. We should just tell Mom and Dad if we want to come back in. We shouldn't lie about it."

"But I want Mom to be proud of me. A real Star Scout doesn't give up. You can stay out here if you want; I'm going inside. If you don't want to freeze, come with us. I just don't want you to wish you had come."

"Well maybe you're not a real Star Scout. I'm staying out here."

"If that's what you want. Come on, Maddie," I said and walked toward the house.

Zelena said, "Wait. I'll go."

"I knew you would come around. I'm glad you decided to come; plus you have a fear of the dark. I wouldn't want you to come inside screaming. Remember that camping trip where you ran inside Mom and Dad's tent and slept with them because you were scared? Or was that me?"

We all went inside. Maddie slept with Zelena while I slept in my own bed. I would have slept with Maddie, but I'm known to sleepwalk and sleep talk sometimes. It felt so good to sleep in my bed, but I felt a little guilty about sneaking inside, and pressuring Zelena into also going inside.

It was eight o'clock and time to sneak outside. While we were sneaking outside, I could tell Zelena had hardly gotten any rest, and she looked a little depressed and talked less than usual. When we went into the tent there was a furry gray creature with a tail, and black patches around his eyes. Was it a dog?

"That's a raccoon!" Zelena exclaimed.

The raccoon woke up, and started to attack us. We ran

out screaming, and went back inside.

Maddie asked, "How did it get in? There's a fence."

Then I remembered that I didn't lock the gate when I had unlocked it to get the Frisbee.

I confessed, "Um, I sort of left the gate open when I used it to get the Frisbee."

"What?!" they both yelled.

"I'm sorry. I forgot."

Maddie said, "We have to get your parents!"

Zelena volunteered, "I'll get them. I should have stayed out there."

"It's not your fault, Zelena. It's mine. I'll tell them."

"No, I'll tell them."

"Let's tell them together."

Zelena and I yelled, "MOM! DAD!"

Mom and Dad ran out of their bedroom in their pajamas and hair undone.

"What happened?!" Dad yelled.

I answered, "A raccoon got in the tent."

"What? Are you guys OK? When did it get in?"

I said, "We're fine. It must have gotten in five minutes ago. We came in to brush our teeth, and when we came back out, the raccoon was in the tent." I felt a little bad for not telling the truth.

"I'll go get it out," Dad said. "Wait. Raccoons come out at night. It had to have gone into the tent way before five minutes ago. What's going on?"

"OK. I accidently left the gate open, and we went inside because we were cold. I also pressured Zelena into coming inside; sorry Zelena. Then we came back out, and there was a raccoon in the tent. We're sorry."

"We'll deal with this later. I have to get the raccoon out first. And I'm disappointed in both of you, Zoey and Zelena," Dad said then went outside.

The raccoon was already gone, so all he had to do was close the gate. I didn't get punished, but my parents made Maddie go home early, because our parents wanted to have a talk with us. I told them that I didn't tell them I wanted to go inside, because I wanted Mom to be proud of me. Mom told me in her first camping trip, she fell on a hike and twisted her ankle. Becoming a diamond Scout apparently cannot happen overnight. I realized I had a very long way to go.

10

News

IT was finally Monday! The day of my first Star Scout meeting! I would meet my Mom's old Scout master, Ms. June, get my Scout uniform, and meet my fellow bronze Scouts! I couldn't wait! I couldn't contain my excitement! All of that was ruined in science class when we had to work on a boring project with a partner. I didn't know anyone in science class, so I didn't have a partner until Meg came up to me with a smile and said, "Hello Zoey, need a partner?"

Meg was sweet. But she was also skinny, had round glasses, wore overalls, and one of her front teeth was sticking out. She was the smartest kid in our class, though, and could use a friend. She also was polite and nice, so I thought maybe I'd take her as a partner. Plus, she would be hurt if I said no; she may seem boring, and a slight bit nerdy due to her appearance, but it's not like she'd be my best friend, just *A* friend.

I said, "Sure, let's be partners. I don't know many people in this class, so thanks. Zelena my twin sister is in advanced biology classes; my other friend Maddie went to this class earlier than me. Maddie and I had art class together, but that was the only one."

"OK," Meg said, still smiling.

She actually was a pretty good partner. She was quiet, because she said we shouldn't talk in class, but she did most of the hard work on our science project. In fact, our teacher was impressed with our work, so maybe Meg and I made a good team.

After science was lunch. Good. I was starving. I was about to sit at my normal table with Sarah, Zelena, Chloe, and Maddie but saw Meg waving at me. Meg was sitting alone, which made me kind of feel bad for her. I waved a shy wave back, hoping no one would notice me. As much as I liked Meg, if Chloe found out I was "friends" with Meg, she would no longer sit with me, which I was fine with, except Sarah would go along with Chloe and no longer be my best friend.

Meg screamed over the noise, "ZOEY SONG! COME HERE!"

The noise quieted down for a second, and everyone watched me walk over to Meg, which seemed like hours. I quietly put my tray down and sat next to Meg. Then everyone continued talking, and no one stared at me. I started to nibble at my pizza, suddenly less hungry.

"Hi, Zoey," Meg said. "I heard you're doing Star Scouts.

So am I. Sorry I didn't get to talk to you about this earlier. I didn't want to get in trouble for talking. Anyway, you must be starting out on bronze Scout. Unless you went to another troop, but there aren't that many other Star Scout troops. I'm also a bronze Scout. I just started last month. I thought if I made it to diamond scout, it would improve my college resume."

I didn't know Meg also wanted to become a diamond scout. I said, "I also want to become a diamond Scout. I love diamonds. My parents once got me a diamond necklace; I have a bracelet that says my name on it; it can only be taken off by a key; my Mom has the key and won't unlock it until my birthday."

After chatting with Meg for a few minutes I forgot about Chloe and Sarah, and found out Meg and I were more alike than I thought. Meg also was having a little trouble with her dreams of being a diamond Scout. She was trying to earn her cooking badge the week before but burned all of her spaghetti. I told her I'd help with her cooking badge, and that I had just the meal for her to cook.

Maddie came up to our table. "Hi Zoey, why aren't you sitting with us?"

"Oh," I remembered. "I decided to sit with Meg. I'm sorry, I'll sit with you tomorrow-"

Then Meg interrupted me. "We can sit with you. It's kind of weird sitting at a table with only two people."

"You don't have to-"

"Nonsense," Meg interrupted me again. "I'm perfectly fine with sitting with your friends. So what if some of them may be messy eaters. I watch my little brother eat all the time." She walked with Maddie to my usual table.

When we walked over to the table, Chloe took one look at Meg and was disgusted. Uh oh. Just what I had feared. Meg was about to take a seat next to Chloe when Zelena said, "I know you. You're Meg. Aren't you in my advanced social studies class and my advanced algebra class?"

"Yep," Meg said with a hint of pride in her voice. "That's me. You're Zelena. It's nice to see you again."

"You too. These are my friends. Maddie, Sarah, and Chloe."

"Nice to meet you. You must be the Chloe who stars in all of those school plays. You're really good at acting," Meg said and sat down next to Chloe.

Chloe suddenly smiled and said, "Thanks, I've starred in five plays since first grade."

After Meg and Chloe's friendly chat, Chloe seemed like she liked Meg. There was something about Meg that made you like her. Maybe it was her cute quirkiness, her smile, or her outgoingness, but whatever it was, it just made you like her.

Later that day I went to the Scout hut for my first Star Scout meeting. Our meeting took place in the Scout hut, which was a log cabin that had a huge front porch. There were tall evergreens outside and birds chirping in the trees. Inside the hut were tables and a podium. Behind the podium was a lady in her twenties with bright yellow hair in a bun; it was even brighter than my hair when I had dyed it. Besides her hair, nothing was really cheerful about her. She had dark brown eyes that looked into your soul with a frown. She also had a big mole on her face. Was this the Scoutmaster? What happened to Ms. June?

I asked Mom who was next to me, "Where's Ms. June? What happened to her? I was looking forward to meeting her."

"Oh, I'm sorry honey. I forgot to tell you, she retired. They have a new one named... I can't remember her name. Well anyway, bye, and have a good time." Mom left.

Oh no. I was left with a grumpy Scoutmaster. At least I'd have Carly, who was wearing her hair in a braid for a change, and was smiling. I sat next to Meg, who was sitting by herself.

"Hi Meg, nice to see you-"

The lady with yellow hair interrupted me. I had been interrupted quite a bit that day. She said, "QUIET DOWN!" The troop was completely silent. "We have a new girl! Get up here, new girl!" the lady demanded.

I slowly walked up to the podium with fear.

"Hello," the lady said with a fake smile. "I'm Ms. Galifinakis, but everyone calls me Ms. Sunshine. Tell us your name."

"Hi Ms. um, Galiflicactus, I mean Ms. Galiflygacis, uh, Ms. Galificus. I'm Zoey."

"It's Galifinakis and sit down now; we have important business to discuss."

Ms. Gali-flick-napkins, or Ms. Sunshine did not deserve her nickname. It should have been Grumpyfinakis. After Ms. Gali-flu-sackis (or whatever her name was) introduced me, I sat next to Meg again.

Ms. Sunshine said, "OK, here's the news. We have a new volunteer to help, which we could use a lot of around here. Her name's Carly. The next news is we're making birdhouses tonight. The last news is we're going camping at a wildlife trail on Friday at five. We'll stay there until Sunday afternoon. Two people will be in one tent, and one of the two people will have to bring a tent, or else the both of you will be sleeping *without* any tent. I will choose the tent mates. Zoey and Meg-"

Great. Me, quirky Meg, responsible Carly, my crazy Scout master, and the rest of my Scout troop, would be stuck in the wilderness together. What could go wrong?

11

Camping

ON Friday at five o'clock, my parents and Zelena dropped me off at the Scout hut. We piled on the bus as fast as we could, because Ms. Sunshine wanted us to hurry.

She yelled, "Faster! FASTER! Not *slower*, Olivia Morgan!"

Everyone started talking after the bus took off, which made a little noise.

Ms. Sunshine yelled, "STOP MAKING NOISE! You're distracting the bus driver!"

We had to whisper to each other, so I whispered to Meg, "Her nickname should have been Ms. Grumpyfinakis."

The bus ride was finally over. It was only an hour but seemed like forever, because we had to whisper, and I hate whispering. Meg did tell me some interesting things about herself, though. She told me she enjoyed acting and was once in a local commercial for pickles. She was "Dancing Pickle Number Three". We became pretty good friends by the time we reached Wildlife Trail.

We were about to get off the bus when Ms. Grumpyfinakis yelled, "EVERYONE! Leave the bus in a calm and orderly fashion!"

Meg whispered, "Ms. Sunshine needs to leave the bus in a calm and orderly fashion." I agreed.

After we got off the bus, and grabbed our luggage, we walked a mile to the place where we would put up our tents. When we tried to put the tent up, Meg and I ended up with the tent caught on top of us. Carly showed up and laughed at us.

I said, "Please help us, Carly. We were arguing over how to put up the tent. Then we ended up with the tent on top of us somehow. At least we didn't forget our tent; Ally and Mindy already did that."

"I'll get you both out," Carly said.

Carly got the tent off of us, and showed us how to pitch a tent the right way. After we had everything set up, it was dinnertime. I was starving, like usual. I ran to the mess hall where dinner would be served.

Ms. Sunshine handed me a piece of meat on a stick and said, "Get your spam on a stick! Then go and cook it at the campfire!"

I went outside to the campfire and threw my spam on a stick into the fire. No matter how hungry I was, I would not eat spam on a stick. I went to bed starving, but I was okay. I was used to being sent to bed with no dinner.

I suddenly woke up to a hoarse and whiny voice yelling, "GET UP."

I rubbed my eyes then went outside. It was still dark, so dark I could still see the moon and the stars. Meg was already awake and outside.

Ms. Sunshine said, "There you are, Zoey! Did you forget you have to cook breakfast for the entire troop?"

"No ma'am," I said. "I just thought we wouldn't have to get up so early to make it."

"Yeah, well you *do*. Now chop, chop! I'm starving! I didn't get to have dinner last night. You girls ate all of my Spams on sticks! I guess it was a big hit. Maybe I'll make it again tonight. Although, one of the girls got a stomachache. Why are you girls still standing there?"

Meg and I ran to the mess hall's kitchen and quickly whipped up some of my chocolate pancakes. I dropped a couple pancakes on the floor but picked them up and put them on the griddle again. Ms. Sunshine was impressed; she even gave Meg and me our cooking badges, even though she ate one I dropped on the floor (That'll be our secret.)

It was raining that morning, but Ms. Sunshine still wanted us to hike four miles! I had brought my rain boots, though, and my gray hoodie. I put the hood of my hoodie up and walked outside in the pouring rain. We went on the trail that had a dirt path. The dirt had turned into mud. Every steep we took, my rain boots would sink into the mud.

"Pick up the pace!" Ms. Sunshine yelled to me, because I was in the back of the line of girls hiking.

Everyone moaned, whined, and complained, even Carly! We started hiking in some green plants, which reached my legs, and tickled them, which made me itch. Then, my whole body itched. I was scratching as fast as I could. Every time I scratched my leg, I wanted to scratch my arms. I looked down at my legs, and they had a rash!

After the miserable four-mile hike, everyone was itchy. I had had enough. I was going into Ms. Sunshine's tent to ask her about our rashes.

I said, "Excuse me, Ms. Sunshine. I'm so itchy. I've never been this itchy; help me please! What's happening?! My skin's almost as red as my hair!"

"Why are you in my tent?" Ms. Sunshine demanded.

Then Hailey, one of my fellow Scouts, went into the tent. She said, "Oh, I'll tell you what's happening."

"Sure, how about everyone come into my tent. Let's make it a party. Woopdie do!"

Hailey said, "We have poison ivy. My dad's a doctor, and he says to use this lotion stuff to help the itching. I have some in my first aid kit. I'll go get it." She ran to her tent.

I asked Ms. Sunshine, "How did you not know we were walking in poison ivy? Didn't you start itching and wonder what was itching you? That stuff was killing me!"

"I thought we were walking in clovers. I probably shouldn't have lain down in what I thought was clovers. Anyway, how was I supposed to know? I've never seen poison ivy."

Hailey brought back something that looked like pink lotion. When she rubbed it on me, I was pink! In fact, the whole troop had it applied, so the whole troop was pink! I wasn't that itchy anymore.

The rain finally stopped, and we were able to get in the pool, but we were already wet. I was excited to swim at first, but then Ms. Sunshine told us to swim one hundred laps, nonstop. She lay back on a lounge chair, drank lemonade, and read a fashion magazine while we were struggling to keep our heads above water.

We had spam on a stick for dinner *again*. This time I gave my spam to Meg, who threw the spam into the fire.

I was about to go to my tent when Carly stood up and said, "Excuse me! Attention!" but everyone was still making noise.

Ms. Sunshine yelled, "SILENCE!" which quieted everyone down.

"Now that I have your attention, I have some good news to share with you all. I have decided to let the troop have S'mores, because of your hard work."

Ms. Sunshine brought out graham crackers, chocolate bars, and marshmallows. I ate five, because I didn't have dinner.

At midnight, I woke up at some loud yelling. I looked at Meg, who was also awake.

I said, "What's that yelling? I didn't hear that yelling yesterday? Is it a raccoon!?"

"No, it's Ms. Sunshine. She sleep screams," Meg explained.

At six o'clock, everyone woke up to a very rainy morning. I hadn't gone back to sleep after hearing Ms. Sunshine sleep screaming, so I was really tired, and immediately Ms. Sunshine forced us to do something outside.

Hailey said, "Like what? It's raining."

"Then just play tag!" Ms. Sunshine yelled.

I said, "OK. I do like to run, but I don't like tag. I used to love hide-n-seek, but when I was ten I hid for two hours; they told me they stopped looking. I was a little mad at them but forgave them. Like how I forgave you for not knowing we were hiking in poison ivy. Thank goodness you had that pink lotion, Hailey. I think I'll have to reapply it soon; maybe in two hours."

The whole troop went into a field near our tents. It had giant mud puddles throughout the field, and it was raining, so it was hard to see anything.

Camilla, another one of my troop members, stood in the middle of the field and said, "Attention! Who wants to be it?"

Camilla always was the leader of the group, so when no one raised her hand, she said, "I guess I'll be it."

"Wait!" I said, "I'll be it!" Even though I wasn't the biggest fan of tag, I still was a good runner.

"OK," Camilla said. "Get ready, set, go!"

I started running, and tried to catch Camilla, but she was super fast. So instead, I chased after Meg. Meg looked like she was an okay runner, but when I chased after she gave it her all and ran across the field. I gathered all my energy and charged at Meg, I was a foot away. Yes! Yes! No! Ah! I fell in a huge mud puddle, that I didn't pay attention to, because I had used all my energy on catching Meg. Splat! Mud was all over me. The worst part was Ms. Sunshine didn't let me clean up, because we were about to leave. The mud was so disgusting, no one sat next to me on the bus. I had cooked breakfast for tons of ungrateful girls, had dodged spam sticks, had listened to Ms. Grump-i-lumpy scream sleep, had mud caked all over my body with no one to talk to on the bus... *AND* I was nowhere close to reaching diamond Scout.

12

Movies and Secrets

ONE bright and sunny afternoon, Maddie, Zelena, and I were hanging out at my house. We did what every kid does on a day like that: watch T.V.

Maddie asked, "What should we watch?"

Zelena suggested, "How about 'Dr. Nelson's Science Show'?"

"No way!" I said, "Let's watch something we'll all like, like 'The Bethany Carson Show'."

"I love that show!" Maddie exclaimed.

"Um, what is it?" asked Zelena.

I said, "Zelena dear, you don't know what 'The Bethany Carson Show' is?" Zelena shook her head. "OK, it's a talk show that stars the famous singer/actress, Bethany Carson. She gives reviews of movies, and her opinions on celebrities and music. It's a really great show. She saved Maddie and me from seeing 'Crazy Chimpanzees'."

"It's true," Maddie agreed.

"Alright, let's watch it."

I turned the channel to "The Bethany Carson Show".

Bethany said, "Hello, it's Bethany Carson again. Today I'm reviewing a popular new movie called, 'Attack of the Killer Zombies'. I've seen the movie, and let me tell you it's extremely realistic, and make sure to be prepared for violence if you're going to see it. It is an *AMAZING* movie, though, and I can see why it's the number one movie in the world. Here's a preview, to let you see a little bit of its amazingness."

A trailer of "Attack of the Killer Zombies" appeared on the screen. It was amazing! I had to go see it.

"Let's go see that! It looks awesome! But wait. It's rated PG-13, and we're not even 12 yet. We could get my parents to take us, but my parents would never let me see a movie like that. Maybe Carly! No wait; she's too responsible to let us do that," I said.

"Hmmm," Maddie replied. "People say I look and act just like my mom, so I guess I look pretty mature. I could probably pass as an adult, and I could buy us all three tickets."

I looked at short Maddie and said, "I'm not sure. You're a little short to pass as a grown up. And you and your mom aren't the same. She talks in an English accent. Plus I don't think she likes my mom that much."

Zelena warned, "We shouldn't go to a PG-13 movie. It's not right."

"But everyone in school has seen it," Maddie insisted before growing a crafty grin. "Wait. I know how we can see 'Attack of the Killer Zombies'. We buy tickets to a G-rated movie, like, um, 'Crazy Chimpanzees', but then we sneak into 'Attack of the Killer Zombies' instead."

I high-fived Maddie. "Great idea! I've taught you well. I can't wait to see a PG-13 movie by myself. Zach has been rubbing it in my face since he's old enough. He got to see the movie, 'Rein of the Evil Mummies' last month. I wanted to see it, but Mom won't let me. I kind of understand why; one of the stunt doubles broke both of their arms while making it. They had to delete that scene; which was OK because it wasn't an *important* scene, the producers say. Tell that to the person with two broken arms. I heard this from an episode of 'The Bethany Carson Show'."

Zelena said, "I don't think we should do this, guys, but I kind of do want to see that movie. It has incredible special effects I hear."

"Then you're in?" Maddie asked.

"I'm in."

"Yes!" I exclaimed. "Then it's settled. Let's go right now; I'll ask our parents. You can ask your parents, Maddie. Just remember. We're gonna say we're going to see 'Crazy Chimpanzees'. I originally thought the movie would be funny, but Bethany Carson said it was just two hours of chimpanzee shenanigans."

I found Mom in her room folding laundry. "Hi, Mom. I was wondering if you'd let Zelena and I see the movie, the movie, uh, 'Crazy Chimpanzees' with Maddie. Um, it, it turns out that, that Bethany Carson's o...opinion about the movie ch...anged. She saw the, the movie again and, and it turns out it, it has a great um, um, uh, sub, sub, subtext."

"Um, OK." Mom said. "Have a nice time, I guess."

"Th...thank you, you, M..M..Mom."

I quickly escaped my Mom's room before I spilled the secret. Hopefully I'd be able to keep the secret after I saw the movie. Or else it would be no dinner for a week, and I don't know if even I could go that long without eating.

Maddie's mom drove us to the theatre. We walked inside to the ticket booth. My legs started trembling, my lips quivering, and my arms shaking.

The man at the ticket booth said, "Next!" It was our turn. Would I give the secret away? I gave the man the money for all of our tickets with my shaky hand, then said, "Th..three t.t..tickets to 'C.C.Crazy Ch..Chimpanzees'." Then I suddenly spoke random words as usual. "Have you ever seen 'Attack of the Killer Zombies'? Did you like it? Let's go see it sometime. Let's go see it with our parents. Well, not our parents. We're not sisters. Well actually Zelena and I are sisters. But Maddie isn't my sister, or Zelena's sister. Maddie and I are best friends, though, and best friends are like sisters, but not sister sisters. Now what about those tickets? Let's get popcorn after we get those tickets."

The man handed us our tickets and raised his eyebrow. "Here are your tickets. Enjoy the movie. Next!"

After we got our popcorn, we snuck into the stadium showing "Attack of the Killer Zombies". Bethany Carson was right. It was *extremely* realistic. Usually I was alright with seeing blood, by pretending it was ketchup, but this wasn't ketchup blood. It was the scariest movie ever! Although I wouldn't have known, except for the first five minutes, I felt like I had my eyes closed for the entire movie.

When the movie was over, we rushed out of the theatre. While we were running past the ticket booth, the man at the ticket booth looked at us suspiciously. Maddie's Mom was going to pick us up, but she wasn't there yet.

Zelena said, "Why did you talk me into seeing that movie?"

"We didn't. You decided," I pointed out. "I'm sorry, I didn't know it would be so scary. But it wasn't my fault you agreed to see it. At least I'm not making you see the sequel or 'Attack of the Killer Mummies'."

Zelena walked away angrily.

"Wait, Zelena!" I yelled.

It wasn't my fault. Zelena had agreed to see that movie, so why was she really mad? There was more trouble than Zelena being mad at me. I still had to keep the secret that I went to a PG-13 movie without an adult. And keeping that secret would not be easy. After Mrs. Jones dropped me home, Mom was watching the news. She looked up at me with judgmental eyes staring into my soul. My heart began to beat fast, then faster, and faster.

My Mom smiled then said, "Hi Zoey. How were those crazy chimpanzees?"

I couldn't believe it! Did my Mom know about the movie? She had to know, or she wouldn't be acting so suspicious.

I tried to act calm, and change the subject. "It was awesome! I loved it! So funny! Great subtext! I'm hungry; I should have eaten more popcorn at the theatre. What's for dinner? I remember: chicken. Don't you love chicken? Chicken pot pie, teriyaki chicken, eggs, chickens do so much for us." Then I almost blurted out the secret. I had to put my hand over my mouth while I said, "By the way I saw 'Attack of the Killer Zombies'."

My Mom said, "What did you say? I couldn't understand you."

"It was awesome! I loved it! So funny! Great subtext! I'm hungry, I should have eaten-"

"No, the last part."

I had to make up something. I couldn't let my Mom know I saw 'Attack of the Killer Zombies'. I said, "Um, uh, I said, yesterday I saw a pack of my favorite gummies. Yah that's what I said. I didn't say something else. That would be weird. That would be crazy, like crazy chimpanzee crazy. Which is the name of the movie that I definitely saw. I didn't go and buy tickets for it, then go see another movie rated PG-13. Well, I have to go do... homework."

I hate homework, but I had to get away from my Mom, before I blurted out the secret.

Mom stopped me. "Wait. Where's Zelena?"

I quickly thought up a lie to say about why Zelena

wasn't there. "Um, well, Zelena decided to run home from the theatre, for practice for track and field. Now I have to go do homework, those negative and positive numbers won't multiply themselves."

"OK, Zoey."

At dinner it was like everyone was staring at me. I tried not to pay attention, looking down at my dinner.

Dad asked, "So, how was everyone's day?"

I couldn't stand it! I had to say something! "OK, stop grilling me!" I said. "I went to see 'Attack of the Killer Zombies'! The movie's rated PG-13, so I bought tickets to 'Crazy Chimpanzees', which is rated G, but went to the theatre showing 'Attack of the Killer Zombies' instead. I'm so sorry! Zelena and Maddie also saw it. I'll go to bed right now. I know the drill."

My parents called Maddie's mom and told her about the movie. They gave Zelena and me a speech about PG-13 movies. They said there was a reason why some movies are PG-13 and we shouldn't do something we know they wouldn't approve of. Trust me, I'd never see a PG-13 movie again. Zelena was grounded for a week, and since the grounding punishment wasn't working out for me, my parents made me clean the bathrooms and Zach's room. Ewe! Zach had a collection of smelly socks, and moldy food he forgot to throw away in his room.

Zelena said she was sorry for blaming me for her seeing the movie. It turned out she was mad at herself for doing something so wrong. She said she just wanted to be cool and see a scary movie like everyone else at school. I guess she just wanted to fit in, like Zach. I felt bad for Zelena and apologized for coming up with the idea of seeing 'Attack of the Killer Zombies'. Anyway, I learned my lesson. I had nightmares about zombies for weeks.

13

The Brownie Business

I was waiting for Star Scouts to begin. I loved Star Scouts and already had three badges. My cooking badge. My animal lover badge. My public speaking badge. Despite my crazy Scoutmaster, Ms. Sunshine, who Meg and I secretly called Ms. Grumpyfinakis, activities at Scouts were fun. Like learning to light a fire. You'll never guess what you use: matches! Instead of twigs, you use matches! It's incredible, isn't it? Anyway, the meeting finally started. I couldn't wait to know what fun surprises awaited me.

Ms. Sunshine yelled, "Quiet! Silence!" The troop quieted down as usual. "I have an announcement. We are going to start selling brownies. On Saturday, we will sell brownies at 'The Brownie Bakery'. Don't worry, I checked. It's legal, or is it illegal, I don't remember. But just in case wear your best running shoes, and bring pepper spray. The money we raise will go to 'Help Houston Stay Clean'. You all will be split up in groups of four, and each group will bake brownies to sell together. Split into groups yourselves, I no longer care if you aren't paired up with your BFFs. At least I won't be to blame."

I immediately looked at Meg and said, "Wanna be partners? I'm a pretty good chef. Remember those pancakes we made on that camping trip. That was the day we all got poison ivy. We had to put that pink stuff on us. I used to dream of having pink skin, but I stopped when we had to put that stuff on."

"Sure, let's be partners. We need two more partners though," Meg reminded me.

We looked around the room, and everyone already had a partner. Then Carly came walking up with a smile.

"Hi girls," Carly said. "Do you have your group yet?"

"No, everyone already has a partner. We need two more. Hey that's funny, just like how I need to do two more chores to complete my chores for the week. I have to clean my side of the room, and vacuum the living room. I like hearing the noise while I vacuum, so I like vacuuming the living room, but I don't like cleaning my room. But I know that Zelena will clean my side of the room when she cleans hers. She hates seeing her side look so good while mine looks like a pig lives in it. Although Zelena tells me that pigs are actually really clean animals, so technically Zelena's side looks like a pig lives in it, right?"

Carly shook her head and said, "I can be a partner, but

we still need one more."

"Let's ask Ms. Grumpyfinakis about it," Meg said.

"Alright, wait, Ms. Grumpyfinakis?"

"Long story. Ms. Sunshine!" Meg yelled.

Ms. Sunshine slowly strolled over to us and rolled her eyes. "What do you want now? And how dare one of you shout at me! I do a lot for you girls!"

I said, "Sorry. That was Meg. She wanted to tell you that we only have three people in one group. Is there anyone else who can be our partner? But please don't make it Mindy Brown. Rumor has it that she doesn't wash her hands, and I don't want to be responsible for brownies that were made by unwashed hands."

"Well, there is one person who doesn't have a partner," Ms. Sunshine said.

"Really, who?" Carly asked.

"Me." Ms. Sunshine smiled.

"You!" Carly, Meg, and I exclaimed with shock.

"Yes me! I actually think it would be fun. I never got my cooking badge."

"I wonder why, considering her success with spam on a

stick," Meg whispered to me.

"Quiet! Now we're going to work at your house, Zoey, tomorrow at four o'clock."

"But-"

Ms. Sunshine interrupted me, "NO buts about it! Now everyone knows where Zoey's house is, that awkward looking one story blue house in Glen Clove? Bye! See y'all tomorrow!"

When Mom picked me up, I told her Ms. Sunshine, Carly, Meg, and I had to bake brownies at our house the next day. Mom told me how to make them and left a recipe out on the kitchen counter. I didn't pay attention though; if I was as good at baking brownies as I was at making pancakes, I'd do fine.

I was excited to get to cook with Carly again. I expected it to be lots of fun. While I was waiting for everyone to show up, I looked at the recipe card. I wouldn't need a recipe, would I? No, I wouldn't. So I tossed the recipe into the trash where it belonged.

Finally everyone showed up ready to bake. Carly was wearing a new pink, ruffled apron. I showed everyone to the kitchen, where I already had the ingredients out; flour, an egg, sugar, and most importantly, chocolate milk.

Carly yelled, "These are the ingredients?! Didn't your

Mom mention a recipe?"

"Nope, no recipe here," I lied, then said, "but I have a great recipe in my mind; one egg, a fourth of a cup of flour, three cups of sugar, and two glasses of chocolate milk. Loosen up Carly, you don't have to follow someone else's recipe to do something right. You should know that, you're a chef."

"That's way too much sugar! And just chocolate milk won't make it have enough chocolate!"

"Fine! I'll add the entire carton then! You better just stay out of this if you're going to disagree with everything. You may be the chef, but this is mainly my project and Meg's project. You're just here to make sure we don't burn the house down."

"I'm leaving." Carly left.

Good. Now we could do what we wanted without Carly bossing us around. We made four batches of brownies, and I was about to put them in the oven.

But Ms. Sunshine yelled, "Stop! You girls shouldn't be around an oven. Let me do it!"

"OK," I said. "Come on Meg. Let's go watch 'The Bethany Carson Show'. She's reviewing some band called 'Dark Shadows'-"

"'Dark Shadows'!" Ms. Sunshine yelled. "I love them!

And I love Bethany Carson! This is perfect. Wait for me, I'll be in there in a jiffy."

"Alright," Meg said.

Meg and I went into the living room, and Ms. Sunshine came in, literally, in a jiffy. I turned on the show while Ms. Sunshine yelled, "'Dark Shadows' rules!" When the show came on, Bethany Carson was criticizing 'Dark Shadows'. Then she showed a video of them performing. They were an all boy group, they wore Goth outfits, and one of them had a black spiky Mohawk with orange highlights on top. They also wore makeup and had earrings.

The lyrics in one song were, "You stole my heart! And left me in the dirt! You left me! And hurt me where it hurts! You should be accused of felony! Because of how you yelled at me!"

Instead of drums, it sounded like two garbage can lids being banged together. It was awful! Ms. Sunshine sang along with the lead singer, who was her favorite. His band name was Pickaxe, but his real name was Stanley. When Bethany Carson came back on, she criticized them even more. Ms. Sunshine screamed at her.

"You have no right to talk smack about a great band like 'Dark Shadows'! I'm glad they're not here to see disrespectful people like you!" Ms. Sunshine yelled.

After Bethany finished reviewing "Dark Shadows", I checked on the brownies. Meg came with me. Ms. Sunshine was still steamed up, so Meg didn't want to be left in the same room as her. When we saw the brownies, it looked more like chocolate soup.

"Maybe a few more minutes," Meg suggested.

I agreed. We put them in for fifteen more minutes, but it still looked like soup. So I put them in for fifteen *more* minutes. Then fifteen *MORE* minutes.

Meg kindly said, "I don't think they're going to turn into actual brownies, Zoey. I'm sorry, but you did a terrific job for no recipe."

Ms. Sunshine walked in and said, "She's right. Your recipe probably didn't turn out well."

"Gee, thanks. That helps me feel a lot better," I said.

"You're welcome."

"How could I be so irresponsible? I got rid of Carly, who was the only person who knew what she was doing. But she probably won't help now, because of the way I treated her, and we aren't good at baking brownies. I guess we aren't going to bake brownies then."

"Wait!" Ms. Sunshine said. "I was going to give season passes to 'Fun and Games Amusement Park' to the group that made the most brownies. I paid four hundred dollars for those things! We have to bake the most brownies. If I paid that much for them, I'm using one of them."

"That was the problem," Meg said after inspecting the oven. "You didn't turn the oven on Ms. Sunshine. Anyway, how are we going to bake the most brownies? We can't even bake four batches of them."

"I got it. Let's buy brownies from 'The Brownie Bakery', and say we baked them ourselves," Ms. Sunshine said.

Meg said, "We can't do that! That's cheating, Ms. Sunshine."

"Well..." I tried to decide what to do. "It is, but I want to show Carly we can bake brownies without her. So, let's go to 'The Brownie Bakery'."

I wanted to do the right thing, but it wouldn't hurt to just buy a few nice brownies to show Carly we could bake, would it?

Ms. Sunshine said, "Let's take the 'Dark Shadows' van."

Meg said, "I guess you can drag me along to 'The Brownie Bakery', but what's the 'Dark Shadows' Van?"

"You'll see."

I wondered what Ms. Grumpyfinakis' "Dark Shadows"

van looked like. When we went to my front yard there was a black van with a giant "Dark Shadows" bumper sticker. The van was parked in the driveway and blasted "Dark Shadows" music when she turned on the ignition.

"Why haven't we ever seen this at Scouts?" Meg asked.

"I park it in the garage. I don't want you girls thinking I'm weird or anything. Now get in and let's burn rubber!"

Ms. Sunshine sang along with Pickaxe, aka Stanley. In the first song Stanley sang, "I'm down in the dirt! I'm locked in a cage! Now that you're gone! There's no such thing as happy days!"

After a very long and annoying car ride, we finally reached "The Brownie Bakery". The aroma of freshly baked, homemade, chocolate brownies filled the air with delight. My mouth was watering from only staring at a batch of triple chocolate chunk brownies being pulled out of the oven. These brownies looked fabulous and yummy. No matter how hard we could try, we would never capture the same amount of yumminess as "The Brownie Bakery".

A girl popped up from behind the counter and startled me. She had golden blonde braids, brilliant blue eyes, and was wearing a pink and white chef hat with a matching apron. "Hi!" She smiled. "My name's Cecilia. How may I help you?"

"Well, I'm Ms. Gallifinakis, and we need twelve

chocolate chunk brownies, twelve chocolate peanut butter brownies, and twenty-four original chocolate brownies."

"OK, Ms. um, Galli-tin-cactus, is that right?"

"NO!" Ms. Grumpyfinakis yelled, which made the cashier Cecilia flinch. "It's Galli-fi-nakis."

"Well, Ms. Whatchamacallit, your brownies will be out soon."

Then Olivia, Isabella, Camilla, and Kaitlyn walked in line right behind us. They were a group in the brownie-baking contest for Scouts. *Why were they here?*

I turned around to face them and said, "Hi guys. What are you doing here? Are you buying brownies, or are you getting a drink. If you're getting a drink, I recommend coffee, it doesn't taste good, but it makes you hyper. It will help you stay up all night to cook brownies for the contest. Oh, that's right, you don't know about the contest. The group that makes the most brownies wins four season passes to 'Fun and Games Amusement Park'."

"They weren't supposed to know that!" Ms. Sunshine yelled at me.

Camilla exclaimed, "Seriously?! We just were coming in here to get a batch of brownies for the brownie stand, because we're horrible bakers. But now that you told me that, I'll take um, fifty original chocolate brownies please."

"Yes ma'am," Cecilia said and then handed Ms. Sunshine our brownies. "Here you go Ms. Whatchamacallit, that'll be forty eight dollars, please."

"I'm not finished," Ms. Sunshine said with fire in her eyes. "Twelve more original chocolate brownies, please."

"Yes ma'am."

"Wait a second," Camilla said with the same fire in her eyes as Ms. Sunshine. "*Twenty-four* brownies of the day, please."

"Yes ma'am."

"Not so fast missy. *TWENTY-FIVE* chocolate chip brownies, please."

Camilla and Ms. Sunshine continued buying more and more brownies. Meg and I warned her to stop, because Camilla seemed determined, and when she's determined, nothing gets in her way. But Ms. Sunshine ignored us and told us she was teaching us "good negotiating". Ms. Sunshine finally gave in after buying two hundred brownies. Camilla and her group ended up buying two hundred and one brownies. I felt bad for Ms. Sunshine. I could have tried harder to stop her from spending two hundred dollars on brownies, but it did teach her a lesson about lying.

When we drove the "Dark Shadows" van back to my house, Ms. Sunshine was sobbing and listening to the most sorrowful "Dark Shadows" songs. When we got home we set the boxes of brownies on the kitchen counter and heard a knock at the door. Meg and I went to see who it was. It was Carly!

She said, "Sorry about how I stormed out earlier. I was not even considering your recipe idea, and even though it had a few flaws, I could have helped you with it nicely. Can I still help you?"

I said, "Um, uh, um, uh, well, uh. We um, already fi... finished the, the b..b brownies."

"You did! May I see them?"

Meg winked at me and said, "Yes. But first, do you want to see me tie a knot? I'm working on my knot-tying badge. I'll do it on my shoe, OK?"

"Alright," Carly said.

"I need to go get the brownies prepared," I excused myself.

I really did. I had to put two hundred brownies on plates, and throw away the boxes that said "**The Brownie Bakery**" in bold print. I sure hoped Meg was a slow knot tier.

I yelled, "Ms. Sunshine! Quick! Throw the brownie

boxes away, while I put the brownies on plates. Carly's here!"

"OK," Ms. Sunshine said.

After fifty brownies, I ran out of plates, and used bowls instead, then cups. We were done preparing the brownies when Carly and Meg walked in.

"Good news," Carly said. "I finally untied Meg's shoe lace." She finally saw all the brownies. "Wow, these look amazing. Mind if I try one?"

"Go right ahead," I told Carly. "We worked very hard, so I hope you like them. And trust me very, very, very hard."

Carly ate one and said, "These taste like they were professionally made." Then she saw the trash can overflowing with "The Brownie Bakery" boxes. "Maybe they *were* professionally made. Care to explain?"

I said, "Well, Camilla and the rest of her evil group shoved those boxes in our trash can while we were taking a break so we wouldn't get those season passes to 'Fun and Games Amusement park', because it would make you think we had cheated." Carly rolled her eyes and folded her arms. "OK fine, here's what really happened. Our brownies were a total disaster, and we didn't ask you to help, because of the way I treated you. We were about to give up when Ms. Sunshine decided to go to 'The Brownie Bakery' and buy brownies instead of baking them. We ended up buying two hundred brownies, because Camilla and the rest of her group were also there, and wanted to buy more than us for the contest. I just wanted to prove to you we could bake a simple batch of brownies without you. I'm sorry, I should have let you help me bake the brownies before any of this mess started."

Carly pointed out, "But instead you pushed me away. Well, we can't sell these brownies, and Camilla and her group can't sell their brownies either."

"We can't?!" Ms. Sunshine said. "But I spent six hundred dollars on this little brownie stand thing!"

"Well, that's what you get for lying. The prize should go to a group that actually worked hard and baked the most brownies. Besides, we're supposed to help 'Help Houston Stay Clean' from this brownie sale. That's what it is supposed to be about, but now it's about prizes and showing people you can bake brownies. And also Ms. Sunshine, being a Star Scout master is about teaching young ladies to do the right thing, but you did the exact opposite. You all should be ashamed of yourselves."

I was ashamed of myself. I shouldn't have cared about showing Carly I didn't need her, and I shouldn't have pushed her away, or gone along with Ms. Sunshine's plan.

I apologized, "I'm sorry Carly."

Meg said," Me too."

Ms. Sunshine said, "I never thought I'd say this but, I'm, I'm s..s...s...sorry!" She blurted out.

Carly said, "And I shouldn't have just left the group, because I was mad. How about we invite Camilla's group over, and I'll show you all how to really bake brownies?"

"That'll be great!" I said.

We all baked delicious brownies together, that we would sell at the stand. We only made two batches, but they were the best tasting brownies at the stand. Emily, Hailey, Lucy, and Taylor baked a total of six batches of brownies and won the contest. They honestly deserved it. They were some of the most hard working and advanced girls in the troop, and I even congratulated them.

In the middle of our sale, a policeman was walking past our brownie stand to the bakery. He looked at us weirdly but continued walking. When he walked back out, he had the bakery's owner! Maybe doing a brownie stand in front of "The Brownie Bakery" really was illegal.

The police officer said, "You need a permit to do a bake sale here."

"Run!" Ms. Sunshine yelled. "And use that pepper spray if necessary! To the 'Dark Shadows' van."

The whole troop ran to Ms. Sunshine's van. There were

seventeen people in the van, and I didn't even have a seat.

Meg yelled, "Half of us don't have seats!"

"Don't worry! This isn't the first time I've run from the police with a Star Scout troop! Long story!" Ms. Sunshine yelled while darting to the Scout hut.

Ms. Sunshine was caught, but it turned out she only had to pay a fine for not having a permit. It was originally five hundred dollars, but the police officer lowered it to two hundred and fifty dollars, because we were giving the money to "Help Houston Stay Clean". So Ms. Sunshine ended up spending $850 dollars on our brownie stand. I hope she learned her lesson, but now that you know about Ms. Sunshine, you probably agree with the rest of the troop that it is highly unlikely.

14

Fieldtrip Fun

I skipped into my art class with Maddie by my side. Everything was going fantastic that day. I made pancakes for breakfast, and Mrs. Lewis was too busy to teach us, so we had a substitute who played a movie that had nothing to do with what we were learning about in ELA. It was awesome! My day was going to be even better with the warm, friendly, caring Ms. Crystal teaching my favorite subject, art, and sharing the joy with my best friend.

Maddie and I sat together at our usual table, which was the closest to Ms. Crystal. We both talked during class, and Ms. Crystal noticed it, but she was fine with it, except for when she was talking.

"Hello class. It's great to see you all again," Ms. Crystal greeted with her joyful smile, which seemed a little more joyful than usual. "I have some very special news I think you'll enjoy."

Maddie whispered to me, "Oh boy. Ms. Crystal has special news. My Mom's last special news was she was taking me to the science museum."

We both said, "Boring."

Ms. Crystal told us, "Please, no talking in class."

Then we said, "Yes ma'am."

"Anyway class, my news is that Monday our class is taking a fieldtrip to 'The Tate Gallery of Fine Art'. This certain gallery has works of art from the 1800s. It is owned by Mr. John Tate. His great great grandfather, James Tate, was a famous artist from the 1800s. Many of his paintings are in 'The Tate Gallery of Fine Art' today. We will meet at this classroom, at the normal time of class, and will come back at fourth period. I will pass out permission slips that one of your parents must sign.

Ms. Crystal handed Maddie and me our permission slips. I couldn't believe we were going to an art gallery. It would be fun to see famous paintings in person.

Apparently, Maddie shared the same opinion. She said, "This is going to be so cool. Seeing paintings from so long ago."

"Yah," I said, "I can't wait until Monday. I hope we'll meet Mr. Tate. John Tate, not James Tate. Unless Mr. James Tate is still alive and not a ghost. If he is a ghost, I'm going to try to put my hand through him."

This day really was turning out great. I didn't have

detention! Since I didn't have detention, I got to take the bus instead of having to call my parents to pick me up or having to walk home. When I got home from school I had to ask Mom to sign my permission slip.

I said, "Hi Mom. Could you please sign this permission slip? It's for a fieldtrip to 'The Tate Gallery of Fine Art'. Ms. Crystal says that it has paintings from the 1800s.

"Did they even have paint that long ago? The 1800s were a *long* time ago."

"I'll sign it, and I'm pretty sure they had paint in the 1800s." Mom signed the permission slip. "Please stay with your teacher while you're there. It's a big place."

"Yes ma'am. I hope we'll see the entire gallery while we're there. We're going to miss second and third period. I'm glad we're missing third period; that's my science class, and I don't like science."

I tried to prepare everything I would need for the fieldtrip on Monday. I decided I'd probably get hungry, so I put a chocolate bar in my pocket. That morning at ELA class, Mrs. Lewis talked about boring idioms. This made me want to go on the fieldtrip even more. Finally the bell rang and it was time for the fieldtrip. I ran out of the room and Mrs. Lewis quickly handed me my homework. I ran to my locker and shoved in my homework and books. I then dashed into Art class, where only Ms. Crystal was in the room.

After I waited for ten minutes for the rest of the class to show up, it was time to leave. We all got on the bus and rode to 'The Tate Gallery of Fine Art'.

Before we entered Ms. Crystal said, "Today we will only be seeing the still lives section, because we are about to begin our still lives unit in art."

As Ms. Crystal continued to talk, I whispered to Maddie who was sitting next to me, "Still lives; what's that? I hope it's interesting, like abstract art. Abstract is fun and imaginative, and easy to do. I painted a blue cow for my abstract project, and my Mom said, 'Is that an alien?' when I showed it to her."

Ms. Crystal said, "Excuse me, no talking please."

"Yes ma'am." Maddie and I said.

"Now, let's go see some art, and remember to always stay with your fieldtrip buddy."

Maddie and I were fieldtrip buddies so we walked off from the front of the bus where we were sitting together, and into the gallery. The gallery had signs pointing to different sections. There was a historical paintings section, replicas of famous paintings, and still lives. We led the group to the still lives section, where the first painting we saw was a bowl of fruit. Seriously, a bowl of fruit is considered art? Is this what still lives were, *paintings of fruit*? Maybe so, but the next painting was a vase of roses.

Maddie whispered, "This is not what I expected."

I said, "Yah, I'm tired of looking at fruit and flowers. I can't believe we have to be here for almost two hours! Hey, here's an idea, let's go sneak over to another section. Ms. Crystal won't notice. She's too busy with the other kids, and we'll sneak on the bus before they're on it. Besides, we're fieldtrip buddies, and if I leave the group, so do you."

"Well, I guess. I don't think I can look at another bowl of fruit or vase of flowers."

We both quietly went to the back of the group before sneaking off to the historical paintings. A lot of the paintings were by James Tate. The first painting was a little red farm with crops and animals. It was very realistic; it looked like a photo.

"Wow!" Maddie said. "I don't think I'll ever be an artist if this is how realistic their paintings have to look."

"Yah, this is a lot better than still lives." Then I saw a tag on the painting. "Hey look; you can buy this one for, um, what?!"

Then Maddie asked, "How much? Let me see. Wow!

That's more expensive than my Mom's new refrigerator."

"It's more expensive than my parents' new car! I think; I'm not sure. It's a pretty nice car; it has a television, a radio that actually works, and cup holders for everyone. I couldn't use my cup holder in the last car, because I shoved a cup too big for it into the cup holder and couldn't get it out."

After looking at more and more paintings, I got hungry. I remembered my chocolate bar in my pocket. I reached for it in my pocket but felt melted chocolate. I pulled out my hand, and chocolate was all over it, so I started licking my fingers. When I had licked my entire hand, I reached into my pocket for some more melted chocolate. It was surprisingly good, tasted like chocolate milk with extra chocolate.

As I licked my hand Maddie said, "Wow! Look at this cat painting!"

I looked up and saw an amazing painting of a white fluffy cat that lay down; it looked as if the cat was really there. I had the sudden urge to pet it, so with my chocolate covered hand, I started to place my hand on the painting.

"No! Zoey! You can't touch the paintings with chocolate on your hand!" Maddie yelled.

Even though Maddie had said this, I had already rubbed the cat painting and smudged chocolate all over it. Then I heard footsteps coming from down the hall. *Oh no, was it Ms. Crystal?*

I stared at the painting, then looked at Maddie and said, "Oh no, I'm going to get in trouble. I already am punished, and I don't want to be again. "

A man appeared. He was wearing a tux, and a tag that said JOHN TATE!

Mr. Tate said, "You two kids ruined my great great grandfather's painting!"

Maddie said, "I did it. I was eating a chocolate bar and got chocolate on the painting. I'm sorry."

"No, I did it," I confessed, feeling guilty Maddie had covered for me." *I* got the chocolate bar all over my hands, *I* touched the painting, and *I* ruined the painting. I did it all, and I'm sorry. I take full responsibility."

"Good, then you're going to pay for it." Mr. Tate said.

"But I don't have the money."

"Then you're going to have to get a job here."

"Doing what?"

"You'll see."

Mr. Tate took me to the front and handed me a mop.

"You're a janitor now," Mr. Tate said.

It took me the rest of the fieldtrip to finish mopping. I

wished I hadn't touched the painting. Not only did I have to be a janitor until my sixth grade school year ended, but also I had detention for a month. So did Maddie. Ms. Crystal noticed Maddie and I weren't with the group, so they searched for thirty minutes. When they found us, we got detention.

*

On the bus ride back to school, Maddie was silently looking out the window.

I said, "Maddie, I'm sorry I got us both in trouble. Thanks for taking the blame though. I know you did that just because you're such a great friend."

Maddie said, "You're welcome. I also deserve detention. I should have stopped you from leaving the group instead of going along with you. I'm sorry."

"Thank you. I guess we both deserve to be punished because of my bad idea."

I had to work at the art gallery for the whole day and on weekends! They even got me a janitor jumpsuit! Zach would watch me work and laugh.

He even said one day, "I think you found yourself the perfect job."

I guess I shouldn't have made up those funny jobs for

him. I mopped the floor, cleaned the girls *and* boys bathrooms, and did other gross work while Zach was eating a chocolate bar and making fun of me. Finally after a long morning of work, I had my lunch break.

I had accidently left my lunch at home, so I decided to use my paint supplies. I always brought some to paint a zebra. I ended up painting the best zebra I had ever painted. If only the whole world could see it. Wait, I was working at a famous gallery. *I could tape my painting to the wall.* I knew just the place, where the cat painting used to be. I walked over to the historical paintings section and taped my zebra painting to the wall. I used packing tape, so my painting wouldn't fall off the wall. *Mr. Tate will love it*, I thought.

After my lunch break Zach left for his 'Science Geeks' game club, so I wouldn't have to worry about Zach making clever remarks about my job. After two hours slowly went by, Mr. Tate walked up to me while I was dusting the still lives section's paintings. He did not look happy.

Mr. Tate said, "I saw your painting that you hung. I took it off, and some of the wall paint came off. I'm going to have to fire you. You've already caused enough trouble your first week."

"OK," I said, relieved to not have to work anymore. "But wait, do I have to pay for the painting I ruined?"

"Trust me, your absence is worth more than any amount of money."

I learned two valuable lessons. I would never leave the group on future fieldtrips. Also, I would not bother to solicit my brilliant artwork to the Tate Gallery ever again. I would simply move on to a better gallery with more refined taste.

15

Cotillion

MY mom had invited Chloe and the rest of her family over for dinner one evening. I wasn't very happy. Chloe and I didn't exactly "get along". Chloe had manners, grace, elegance, (and could be a tad annoying). When she came over she was wearing a navy blue dress with a diamond belt around it, along with a pair of sparkly heels that matched the belt, and a white sweater. While I wore a comfy pair of sweat pants, and an oversized "Science Geeks" shirt that Zach had given to me for Christmas.

I said, "Hey Chloe. What do you wanna do? Dinner won't be ready for another thirty minutes. Don't you think lunch at school should be longer than thirty minutes? You end up having to wait in line for ten minutes, if you're buying your lunch. I usually buy my lunch, but if I make my chocolate pancakes the night before, or in the morning I save the leftovers for lunch."

Zelena explained, "What Zoey is trying to say is, hello."

"Oh, good evening," Chloe said. "I brought a jigsaw puzzle of an old cathedral, so we might as well do that."

"Alright, sounds fun," Zelena said.

It did *not* sound fun to me. Chloe dumped out a one thousand-piece puzzle on the small coffee table, which made half the pieces fall off. This definitely didn't look fun or sound fun. Perhaps I could make up an excuse to not do the puzzle.

An excuse popped in my head. I said, "I'm thirsty; I'll go get a drink. Actually, how about I get drinks for all of us? I'll go get us all water. This might take a while, like the thirty minutes until dinner. Have fun with the puzzle. Bye!"

Chloe asks, "Wait. Do you have any cups for special occasions? I've eaten dinner at your house before, and all your normal cups are so casual. Last time, I had to drink out of your Dad's stadium cup."

"Sure. Whatever," I said.

I went into the kitchen where Chloe's Mom, Mrs. James, and my Mom were having a conversation. As I searched for the cups, I overheard them.

Mrs. James said, "I hope cotillion goes well for Chloe. She has only done it once, but it was only a junior cotillion. She has taken ballroom dance lessons before, so she'll certainly excel at that part. I hope this will cheer her up. Some of her old friends from finishing school are also doing it. Chloe has not been very happy since I pulled her out of finishing school; perhaps I will send her back next year."

Good, send her back, I thought, still searching for those hidden cups.

"Cotillion, oh, I've never thought about that for Zoey. I would send Zelena, but I'm afraid she'd end up teaching the class."

"My little Chloe probably will someday."

Cotillion! For me! No way! *And where are those cups?* I thought.

I asked my Mom, "Where are the special cups? Please, please, please! Where are the cups?"

"At least she said please," Mom pointed out.

I said, "Oh, now I remember where the special cups are! I accidentally broke them when Maddie and I were trying to have our own carnival. We were doing that booth where you try to throw a ball into a bottle, and I used our special cups instead of bottles, because we don't have any bottles. Besides, we never use our special occasion cups. Let's just say, it didn't go well."

Mrs. James looked shocked then calmly said, "The cotillion is located on 34 Main Street, for more information please go on the website, www.graceandcharm.com. I assume you will be attending soon."

After dinner, Chloe and her family left. My Mom thanked Mr. and Mrs. James for coming. Then my Mom pulled out her computer and looked at the *Grace and Charm* website. I wasn't exactly sure what a cotillion was, but I knew it was *not* going to be fun if it had something to do with grace, charm, and ballroom dancing.

At school at the lockers, I was talking to Maddie about cotillion. She told me it didn't sound that bad, then the bell rang, and it was time for Mrs. Lewis' class. I quickly ran to class, and sat down at my desk. Behind my desk was an annoying boy named Matthew, who I had known since kindergarten; he was tapping his pencil on his desk and making a "click" sound with his mouth. He had been teasing and irritating me since kindergarten, and, oh yah, pulling my ponytail. He finally stopped tapping his pencil and making sounds with his mouth, thank goodness. Then I felt a hard yank on my head. Ouch! That had to be Matthew, Ponytail-Pulling-Matthew.

I turned around to face Matthew and whispered, "Stop it. You've been doing that to me since kindergarten. When are you going to just stop? You're going to get in trouble one of these days-"

Then Mrs. Lewis said, "No talking in class Zoey! Detention after school."

"Yes ma'am."

In all of Matthew's years of antagonizing me, never once had he ever gotten caught. The teachers probably thought he was a sweet, innocent, harmless little boy. Wrong! He went in for one more yank, this one less painful, but it still hurt. Then he continued tapping his pencil and clicking. Matthew could use cotillion more than me.

After Mom forced me to complete my homework, it was time for cotillion. I didn't understand. *Why did I have to do it but Zelena didn't?* I was almost as well behaved as her. I only "exaggerated" a little while asking for things. For example, Zelena would say, "Could you please pass the salt?" I would say, "Pass the salt! Please! Please! Please! I can't live without it! Don't you care about my happiness?"

Mom drove me to the fancy event place. Entering the "Grace and Charm Cotillion", we were greeted by a lady with a warm smile. She wore diamond earrings and a nice dress with her hair in some fancy up-do.

The lady gracefully walked towards us, then she said, "Hello, I'm Ms. Livingston. It is an honor to be teaching your young lady the art of grace, poise, and elegance. Now, are ya gonna pay with cash, debit, credit, or check?"

"Credit will be fine," Mom said.

"Very well," Ms. Livingston said. "Excuse me, who are you young lady?"

"Me?" I asked. "Zoey, with a y. My dress is uncomfortable; so are these shoes. Why did you make me wear Zelena's clothes, Mom? Zelena is my twin, and yes we look alike. Her hair's slightly shorter though; she got a haircut last week, but I insisted on letting my hair still grow out."

"Well, I'll show you to your partner. He'll be your partner for the rest of the week."

"Bye," Mom said, then left.

Hopefully I'd like my partner, and he won't be annoying. Ms. Livingston led me to the ballroom, then to Ponytail-Pulling-Matthew!

I yelled, "Matthew!"

"Zoey!" he yelled.

"Oh good. You two know each other. You will be partners for the rest of the week," Ms. Livingston said.

Matthew and I yelled, "No!"

Ms. Livingston ignored us and went along with her job. I couldn't believe that Matthew was my partner at cotillion for the rest of the week. What did I do to deserve this?

"Attention class! Good evening, ladies and gentleman. Welcome to cotillion! I'm Ms. Livingston, and I'll be your instructor. Gentleman, please escort your partner to her seat by holding her hand and taking her to your table. Pull out the chair for her, please, and thank you."

Mathew and I said, "EW!"

I closed my eyes and we slightly put our pinkies together; then I opened my eyes and Matthew slid my chair far away from the table. I pushed the chair back and sat across from Matthew. EW! I looked down at my lap, because I didn't want to look him in the eye.

"Please, put your napkins in your lap. Your appetizers shall be out soon. For now, chat amongst yourselves. Compliments will start a conversation quite fine."

I put my napkin in my lap and tried to ignore Ponytail-Pulling-Matthew.

Then he said something. "Hey Zoey, you have, um, your hair, um, smells good, I guess."

Did my hair smell bad?! Did it smell good?! Was he smelling my hair?! What did he mean?!

"I mean... I mean, it, um, looks nice, better than it does in a ponytail."

"Um, thanks. You, um..." I said, trying to figure out a

compliment. "You have, um, a nice, uh, pair of uh, feet."

I shouldn't have said "feet", but it would do. The appetizers finally came. Just in time to stop the awkwardness. I started to eat my salad with my little fork like we were supposed to. I couldn't pick my crouton up with a fork, so I just picked it up with my hand but accidently dropped it under the table, so I went under the table to grab it, and ate it down there.

Ms. Livingston caught me. "A young lady should not be eating under the table."

I said, "Sorry, dropped a crouton. But that's why we have the five-second rule, right? Maybe I should just get back in my seat."

I started to stand up and bonked my head on the table. So instead I grabbed the table to get up, but the tablecloth fell off, along with our silverware and food. I was covered in lettuce and ranch and was extremely embarrassed. Everyone was watching every move I made. I carefully got out from under the table and picked up my chair that had fallen.

"Zoey Song!" Ms. Livingston yelled. "I'm sorry, but I think it would be best if you left for now."

"Yes ma'am," I said.

Mom picked me up and seemed upset.

In the car she said, "I just wanted you to behave for one

night! Was that so much to ask?"

"No ma'am," I said.

"Why did you have to use the five-second rule?"

I really did feel sorry. *Ms. Livingston probably hates me now*, I thought. I'd have to become the best student, so she'd like me again. She'd have to like me.

* * *

At cotillion the next day, I was wearing my Mom's old black dress to look sophisticated. It wasn't exactly my style, but I wanted to look mature and adult-like. I would act with such grace and beauty, and be the best at everything we were going to do. Hopefully my plan would work out well.

When I saw Matthew he was wearing a bright ugly yellow sweater, but I wanted to be polite, so I said, "Good evening Matthew William Peterson. What a lovely day it has been. I absolutely adore that exquisite and characteristic, lovely, cheerful, yellow sweater you're displaying on this fine evening."

Matthew said, "What's up Zoey? Cool funeral dress. Who died?"

I could hardy take Matthew's insult, but I was trying to be a polite lady, and polite ladies don't tackle boys who mistreat them. I only thought about calling him a duck, then quacking while waddling around him.

Then Ms. Livingston walked in and said, "Hello Zoey. It is always a pleasure seeing you."

"As to you, Ms. Livingston. You're looking quite lovely this evening. Not that you don't always look lovely. You just look lovelier, or is lovelier not a word? Wait, you look the same amount as lovely as you always do, so I guess what I'm trying to say is you look lovely like usual. I'll just go sit down now." I was embarrassed I couldn't even give a compliment the right way.

Ms. Livingston said, "Hello, ladies and gentleman. Today we are working on ballroom dancing, which is essential to Friday's dance."

There was a dance on Friday! I had to prove myself at that dance!

Ms. Livingston continued talking. "My star students, Chloe and Alastair, please demonstrate a standard ballroom waltz, please."

Chloe and her handsome partner, Alastair, went to the middle of the room. They demonstrated a perfect dance then curtsied and bowed after the dance. Everyone clapped for them, and our instructor complimented their presence and elegance.

"Does anyone else want to try?" Ms. Livingston asked.

This could be my opportunity for the whole class to cheer and clap for me, and for Ms. Livingston to like me, and for me to be the star student instead of Chloe. *I can't pass up an opportunity like this*, I thought.

"Anyone?" Ms. Livingston asked. I raised my hand and she said, "Oh, fine. Please come up here, Zoey and Matthew."

While we walked up to the middle of the ballroom, Matthew said, "Are you sure about this?"

When we reached the middle I said, "Yes. Now put your left hand above my waist while I put mine on your shoulder, and hold my right hand."

"OK." He rolled his eyes.

Then we got in our positions and began dancing. I felt so graceful while dancing, and dancing with Matthew was, well, pretty good. I don't know how to describe it, but let's just say... he no longer made me want to say "EW". Everything was going fine, great even, until I accidently tripped and fell on my back.

Matthew exclaimed, "Are you okay!" then grabbed my hand and pulled me up.

I said, "Yah, I'm fine."

We walked back to our seats. I couldn't believe I

messed it all up. Ms. Livingston probably didn't like me even more now. I also made a fool of myself in front of everyone. I sat out for the rest of the evening.

After Matthew goofed off near the group of girls and boys slow dancing he walked towards our table. "Hey Zoey. Since Ms. Livingston is gone right now. We don't have to do that boring slow dance stuff. We can do whatever dance we want. Wanna join me?"

"No thanks. I'm not in the mood."

"Come on."

"Fine."

Then I did the robot, and Ms. Livingston walked in. Uh, oh. I got caught. I wasn't sent home, though; she just rolled her eyes and made us sit out for the rest of the class.

Wednesday and Thursday's classes passed by quickly. On Wednesday I finally slowed danced with no accidents, and I learned about manners on Thursday. Friday, the day of the big dance finally came. I wore my red hair in a bun, Zelena's white long dress, and white wedges. Matthew was wearing a black and white tux that he sort of looked handsome in.

Ms. Livingston said, "Our dance shall begin with dinner. Gentlemen please escort your ladies to their seats."

Matthew and I actually held hands this time, and he

pushed the chair back in for me. Then the waiter placed bread and butter on the table. I started to try to put butter on my bread.

"Do you want me to help?" Matthew asked.

"I got it!" I said.

Then I accidently knocked the bread off the table. This time I wasn't going to use the five-second rule. Our entrée was sushi! Yuck! I had never eaten sushi before, but I was aware that it was raw fish! That didn't sound very good to me, but I had to prove I was sophisticated to Ms. Livingston. I picked up a piece with my hand and shoved it in my mouth expecting something disgusting. It was great! A lot better than I had expected. I shoved three more in my mouth.

Then Ms. Livingston said, "Hello Zoey, you better behave the right way. I'm going to the ladies' room, and I don't want any funny business when I'm gone."

"Yes ma'am," I said with three pieces of sushi in my mouth.

"Good," She said then left.

I reached for more sushi, but there was none left. Then I saw the doors to the kitchen open. I had an idea. While Ms. Livingston was gone, I'd sneak into the kitchen and eat all the sushi I wanted. I stood up and started walking towards the kitchen.

Matthew said, "Zoey! Where are you going?"

"I'm going to sneak sushi," I answered. "Do you wanna join me? That is if you liked the sushi. If you didn't, that's weird because of how good sushi is. It's almost as good as my chocolate pancakes. I once opened a pancake business, but it failed; so did my art cart. There was less business, and Maddie and Zelena stopped helping. Zelena got busy with track and field."

Matthew shrugged, "I guess I'll join you."

We snuck into the kitchen, and no one was in it until Chef Moko caught us.

He said, "Ah hah! Caught you two. You know I've heard from Ms. Livingston that you two have been causing trouble around here."

Matthew said, "Hello Chef Moko. Wow! You look great! Doesn't he look great Zoey? Tell him he looks great."

I said, "You look great. Have you lost weight, and did you shave? You look amazing without the beard and mustache, you can really see your handsome mouth better. Look, please don't send us home. I've already been sent home this week."

Of course we were sent home and had to wait outside on a bench for our parents to pick us up.

I said, "Sorry I got us sent home, Matthew. I ruined your week at cotillion."

"No you didn't. I was afraid it would be boring, but thanks to you, it was far from boring."

"Really? Well, you're welcome."

A car pulled up. "That's my ride. I gotta go. See you at school," Matthew said and got inside.

My week at cotillion wasn't so bad. Neither was Matthew. I'd almost call us friends. When I told Mom what happened, she laughed and admitted it was a bad idea to send me to cotillion in the first place. I also learned it didn't matter if Ms. Livingston liked me or not. I began to wonder if maybe it didn't matter what anyone else thought either, for that matter. *Could it be that it only mattered what I thought about myself?*

16

The Graduation Speech

ENCILS were tapping; the class staring at the clock; teachers blabbing on and on about whatever subject they taught. It was the last day of a long year of sixth grade. People couldn't wait for their summer vacations. My parents never said we were going on vacation, but they did say they had special news that they'd tell everyone after our sixth grade graduation. I felt a gentle tug on my ponytail. It was Matthew. Despite our fun at cotillion, he still pulled my ponytail. We had sort of become friends.

Matthew handed me a note. I turned back around and opened it. I was expecting some clever remark about the ugly gray dress my Mom had made me wear, or a funny comment about Mr. Holman's bright pink tie that stuck out with his suit.

Instead it said, "What's up Zoey? Sorry about pulling your ponytail again, you tender headed girls. Anyway, I just wanted to tell you that I'm going to the Bahamas for a month! Have fun staying at home. Ha! Ha!"

I rolled my eyes then stuck my tongue out at him. We may have been friends, but he still hadn't given up on teasing me. The bell rang!

"Class dismissed!" Mr. Holman said over the noise of hundreds of excited students, who ran out in a herd.

Instead of taking the bus, Mom picked up Zelena and me. Mom always did that on the first and last day of school. Zelena jumped into the car with the biggest smile I had ever seen on her face. Usually on the last day of school Zelena would be moping over not getting her "education" until the next grade.

Mom asked, "So, how was the last day of school?"

Before I could say anything, Zelena jumped right in. "Amazing! I was chosen out of the entire school to give a speech at graduation! Can you believe it?"

"I'm so proud of you. You both have worked so hard this year. You getting all As, and Zoey who is starting to get Bs."

"Thank you," Zelena said and coughed really loudly, like she was sick.

"Zelena, are you alright, honey?"

Zelena coughed a little more and said in a scratchy voice, "Yes, I'm fine."

"You don't sound fine. Hopefully you'll feel better by the time you have to give that speech."

Zelena wrote her speech that afternoon, then practiced performing it in front of the bathroom mirror. She practiced and practiced, and the more she practiced, the worse her voice sounded. She was coughing really badly, so Mom told her to get some rest. The next morning she coughed more and more, so Mom took her to the doctor.

When they got back Mom said, "Bad news. Zelena has laryngitis. She can't do her speech."

I said, "Then who's going to do it? Wait, *maybe I could do it*. Ms. Sunshine said I did great on my public speaking badge. That was my favorite badge, except for maybe my cooking badge. I enjoyed cooking those pancakes. I've been thinking of making waffle versions of them, or French toast versions. I think adding a chocolate bar or chocolate chips might make them better. At least Carly suggested that."

Mom said, "Well if you're going to do the speech, sleep in the living room please. I read somewhere online that laryngitis is contagious."

"OK, I like the couch. It's worn out, but it has lots of loose change in it. Once I found a twenty-dollar bill in there. I bought candy with it. I also bought a bag of potato chips with it. By the way, they just came out with a chocolate covered potato chip. Can we get some?"

"Thank you for doing the speech, and no, we are not getting those."

That night I looked over Zelena's speech on the couch. It wasn't a very good speech; kind of boring. Maybe if I said it out loud it would seem better.

I read it out loud. "Good evening students, teachers, and distinguished guests. I am Ze, I mean Zoey Song, and I'm graduating sixth grade. I have learned a lot this past year, besides academics, I've learned about growing up, friendship, and interests I never knew I had. I'd like to give a special thank you to principal Ruff, Mrs. Lewis, Ms. Lawrence, Mr. Malone, Ms. Phillis, and all the other teachers and staff members. Who not only dedicate their lives to children, they dedicate their lives to future doctors, lawyers, and other people who make a change in our lives. Thank you."

It still didn't sound right. I just made a few "tweaks", and trust me, it sounded a lot more interesting. I was sure Zelena would be surprised to hear how much better it sounded, really surprised. So would everyone else.

At graduation the next day, I was ready to give the speech. I thought it would be the best speech ever.

Principal Ruff introduced me. "Hello, I am principal Ruff. There has been a change of plans, because Zelena Song is unable to deliver the speech she wrote. Her sister, Zoey Song, will deliver it for her instead." She walked off stage.

I ran onto the platform and dove right into my speech:

"Good evening students, teachers, and distinguished guests. I am Zoey Song, and I am graduating sixth grade. I made a few tweaks to Zelena's speech, but I believe I'm still getting my sister's point across. I'd like to give a special thank you to principal Ruff for guidance, Mrs. Lewis for teaching us about independent and dependent clauses, Ms. Lawrence for letting us dissect frogs, Mr. Malone for teaching Zelena, Mr. Holman for making us smile with your colorful wardrobe, and all the other teachers and staff members. Who not only dedicate their lives to children, they dedicate their lives to future doctors, lawyers, and other people who make a change in our lives.

However, I have learned much more than just academics. I have learned to be myself. It doesn't matter what others think of you, it only matters what you think of yourself. You should not be ashamed to be different, because in a way, everyone's their own unique individual, and everyone's different in their own special way. So next time you look at someone who may not be exactly like you, think about it this way: what if everyone was the same? That would be pretty boring, so just be you, and let others be themselves.

I have also learned that what you're good at is what society thinks you should do, but it may not be what you love to do. You should choose what you love, because it does not matter what others think, like I said before. For example, everyone wants my cousin Carly to be a doctor, but she actually wants to be a chef. Do you want to give up your dreams just to be like everyone else?

Allowing others to be better at something than you is another lesson I've learned. Like I said, everyone's different, which also means that everyone has his or her own special talents, and you shouldn't be mad at someone just because you don't have the same talents. It's not their fault or your fault. In fact, it's no one's fault, so support others, because wouldn't you want to be supported?

I have learned how important family is and should be. Every family has their flaws, but just like every person's different, every family's different. I would like to thank my Mom who deals with our everyday problems, my Dad who works so hard for us even though he is so unappreciated, my sister, Zelena, who does the right thing no matter what, and my older brother Zach, who uh... keeps things... lighthearted.

I have learned to reach out to everyone no matter who they are, because everyone's different. You also may find out that you have more in common than you may think. But even if you don't learn from each other's differences. Don't you want to experience new and exciting things?

Lastly, accept responsibility for your mistakes. Don't blame them on others. You should be yourself, and being yourself includes telling the truth, owning up to your mistakes, and learning from them. Because as they say, the truth always comes out, and holding it in and not telling it for a long time only makes it worse.

Now, I have concluded one very important thing from all of these lessons I have learned, there are things that teachers teach us, but there are also things that life teaches us, and we should be thankful for both. Thank you."

People were yawning at the beginning of my speech, but everyone applaud at the end. People stood up and cheered. It was amazing. I had surprised them, and they surprised me. In that moment, people actually did like me, and when I least expected it. Even though I preached about not caring what others thought, it was nice to finally be appreciated for something.

My whole family was definitely surprised, especially Zelena. My parents told me how proud they were of me. It was an odd feeling. I wasn't in trouble. After graduation was over, we went to a nice restaurant called "Provino's Pizzeria". We even invited Carly, who attended our graduation. I hoped to hear the exciting news my parents told us about, and even Carly had news. When we got to the restaurant, I was starving and wondering what the news was.

I blurted out, "So what's the big news?!" then stuffed my mouth with rolls so I wouldn't say anything else.

Mom said, "How about you go first, Carly?"

Carly smiled and said, "I have decided to attend a culinary school instead of medical school. Zoey, you have inspired me throughout this year to just take a risk and decide to do what I want to do instead of what other people want me to do. It's better to do something you love rather than what you're good at."

I said, "Really? I told you that. I'm so happy for you! I hope you love culinary school; I know I would."

Carly laughed. "Thanks, and your parents have some more news."

Yes! *This is it*, I thought. I had been dying to know the news the entire week. Carly's news was great, so my parents' news must be even better, I thought.

Dad slowly started, "So the news is... we are going on vacation to Denver, Colorado! We are going there for the rest of summer break."

Zach, and I yelled, "Yay!" We both loved Colorado, even though I had broken my leg there.

Mom said, "There's more. Your Dad got a job offer as the zoo director at 'The Colorado State Zoo', and we're thinking about accepting the offer. That's why we're going for so long. We want to spend some time there to see if we like it, and to house hunt if we decide we want to move there."

I was so shocked, I couldn't see straight and felt my whole body go numb. I turned pale, almost speechless. "Wait... *what*?"

Spicy Meatball Veggie Soup

Meatballs

1 pound ground beef   1 egg beaten

½ cup grated Parmesan cheese   ¼ cup breadcrumbs

2 tablespoons minced onion

Combine all above ingredients.

Form into 1-inch meatballs.

Bake in oven for 30 minutes at 350^0, turning once.

Soup

¼ cup minced onion   14 oz. can beef broth

12oz. can cocktail vegetable juice 15 oz. can crushed tomatoes

2 tablespoons steak sauce   2 tablespoons sugar

2 cups water   2 tablespoons hot sauce

1 bag frozen vegetables- green bean, corn, carrot, pea mix

1 zucchini sliced thick

Add all ingredients to slow cooker.

Heat on low setting.

Add meatballs about 30 minutes left to cook.

Enjoy!

Zoey's Chocolate Pancakes

1/3 cup sugar

1/3 cup light brown sugar

1 ½ cups unbleached flour

1 teaspoon baking soda

½ teaspoon salt

1/3 cup cocoa powder

½ cup chocolate milk

½ cup buttermilk

2 large eggs

1 teaspoon vanilla extract

3 ½ tablespoon vegetable oil.

Mix all wet ingredients together with wire whisk.

In a separate bowl mix together all dry ingredients.

Make a well in dry ingredients.

Pour wet mixture into dry and mix together.

Heat griddle and ladle pancake batter.

Add toasted pecans (without shell).

Flip pancakes when batter forms many bubbles.

Add bananas and whipped cream for special treat!

Don't forget the syrup!

Enjoy!

Carly's Creamy Mac-n-Cheese

16oz elbow noodles

1 stick salted butter

1 teaspoon salt

2 eggs beaten

2 cups shredded sharp cheddar cheese

2 cups mild cheddar cheese

3oz cream cheese cut in cubes

2 cups heavy cream

1 can evaporated milk

½ teaspoon pepper

Boil noodles according to package directions.

Put stick of butter in "Crock Pot".

Add cooked noodles to "Crock Pot".

Add salt, pepper, cream, evaporated milk, eggs, and gently stir.

Add sharp cheddar and 1 cup of mild cheddar cheese and small cubes of cream cheese.

Gently stir.

Top mixture with additional 1 cup mild cheddar cheese.

Cook on high for 30 minutes.

Reduce to low for 2 ½ hours.

Enjoy!

Spam on a Stick

Spam

Fresh pineapple

Skewers

Cut spam into 1-inch cubes.

Cut pineapple into 1-inch cubes.

Put on skewers by alternating.

Put under broiler for 2-3 minutes.

Enjoy! (Or don't)

The Real Star Scout Brownies

½ cup- all-purpose unbleached flour	2 eggs-cold
¾ cup unsweetened cocoa powder	1 ¼ cup granulated sugar
1/8 teaspoon baking soda	1 tablespoon cornstarch
¼ teaspoon salt	1 teaspoon vanilla extract

1 stick + 3 tablespoons unsalted butter

½ cups chocolate chips (milk chocolate or semisweet)

½ cup toasted pecans (optional)

Preheat oven to 325^0

Microwave sugar and butter for 1 minute and 15 seconds.

Stir in vanilla extract and cocoa powder.

Pour contents of this bowl into stand mixer bowl.

Mix on low, add eggs one at a time, until incorporated.

In another bowl, stir flour, baking soda, cornstarch, and salt.

On low, gradually add dry ingredients to mixer bowl.

Mix until no flour pockets remain.

Fold in chocolate chips (and toasted pecans if desired).

Spread brownie batter in 8x8 parchment-lined, greased pan.

Bake for 25-30 minutes or until set.

Remove from oven and allow to cool 30-45 minutes.

Enjoy!

Acknowledgements

I thank God for making this possible and giving me this incredible opportunity. I've trusted in Him throughout this whole process, and known that whatever happened to this book was His plan.

Thank you Mom and Dad (Scott and Jenny Lowery) for supporting me. Thank you Luke; I couldn't ask for better big brother. Thank you to my amazing editor, Mary Claire Branton, who believed in an eleven year-old girl with a dream and then worked tirelessly.

Thank you to cover artist, Ben Curtis Jones, who brilliantly brought Zoey to life. Thank you Summer Jones, for being the perfect Zoey.

ABOUT THE AUTHOR

Mikayla Grace Lowery was born in China on August 23rd, 2005 in a large city called Chong Qing. Someone took her to an orphanage where she stayed for a year. She was blessed beyond measure to be adopted by Scott and Jenny Lowery of Cartersville, Georgia, one month after her first birthday.

Mikayla spent eight years as an award-winning gymnast and began writing short stories when she was nine. She took a step back from gymnastics to focus on becoming a professional child author. She stays active with Cross Fit training and loves all forms of visual art, interior design, and calligraphy. She also plays the piano and is very active at her church. She has been an honor roll student every year in school.

Mikayla Lowery is devoted and never gives up on a goal. She is an amazing little girl with countless supporters. Charlie's Port is developing Mikayla's *Zany Zoey* series, a picture book about birds and publishes her blog that explores the art of writing from a child's viewpoint.